"Would you do s[omething for me before I] go to bed?" Dev as[ked.]

Kristi moved closer, drawn by the entreaty in his face. "What?"

"Don't look so suspicious—it's a harmless request."

He flashed a boyish smile, and she couldn't help but smile back. "What?"

"Will you kiss me good night?"

"You call that harmless?" she asked.

"Perfectly. I won't lay a hand on you. Your dog will make sure of that."

As he linked his hands together behind his back and closed his eyes, Kristi decided one little kiss wouldn't hurt, would it?" "Oh, what the heck." Rising on her toes, she brushed her lips against his. With a coaxing movement, his lips encouraged hers to stay and explore. They felt so warm, so good, she forgot her intention to keep the kiss brief. Giving in to the urge, she twined her hands around his head and pulled it down, reveling in the stimulating sensations.

He was in deep, deep trouble, Dev thought. One taste of her mouth, and he never wanted to let her go. He moaned and held his hands together more tightly, past ready to break his promise not to touch her.

Kristi heard the moan and wondered if it had come from her. Suddenly the full impact of what she was doing stung her like buckshot. Dev wasn't touching her, but she was doing enough touching for both of them. She stepped back and blurted out the first words that came to mind. "You don't call that dangerous? You should declare your lips a lethal weapon."

Dev spoke hoarsely. "And the touch of your lips is enough to make a man go up in smoke. . . ."

WHAT ARE *LOVESWEPT* ROMANCES?

They are stories of true romance and touching emotion. We believe those two very important ingredients are constants in our highly sensual and very believable stories in the *LOVESWEPT* line. Our goal is to give you, the reader, stories of consistently high quality that may sometimes make you laugh, sometimes make you cry, but are always fresh and creative and contain many delightful surprises within their pages.

Most romance fans read an enormous number of books. Those they truly love, they keep. Others may be traded with friends and soon forgotten. We hope that each *LOVESWEPT* romance will be a treasure—a "keeper." We will always try to publish

LOVE STORIES YOU'LL NEVER FORGET
BY AUTHORS YOU'LL ALWAYS REMEMBER

The Editors

Loveswept ®560

Lynne Bryant
Singular Attraction

BANTAM BOOKS

NEW YORK · TORONTO · LONDON · SYDNEY · AUCKLAND

SINGULAR ATTRACTION

A Bantam Book / August 1992

If you would be interested in receiving protective vinyl
covers for your Loveswept books, please write to this address
for information:

Loveswept
Bantam Books
P.O. Box 985
Hicksville, NY 11802

ISBN 0-553-44225-2

Published simultaneously in the United States and Canada

PRINTED IN THE UNITED STATES OF AMERICA

OPM   0 9 8 7 6 5 4 3 2 1

To Iven, who taught me to fly.

One

Kristen Bjornson guided the floatplane into a slow turn and studied the lake below. Larger and deeper than the other lakes that sprinkled the Alaskan tundra, it was rimmed by a rocky hill on one side and a sandy beach on the other. It was also home for family number eighty-four of her Tundra Swan research project.

"There they are," she said to herself, spotting two large white swans, a pen and a cob, swimming gracefully along the shoreline. Following behind, paddling furiously, were five cygnets. "Terrific. All the chicks have survived. So far."

In a few short weeks the family would be migrating south to unknown perils on the wintering range. How many would live to return? she wondered.

With wings flapping, the cob ran across the water, then rose swiftly into the air. Kristi watched his flight, marveling at his grace and power, and imagined what it must feel like to fly. To wing the wind with your own strength and courage. To soar above the earth, bound only by a shadow.

A shadow.

Suddenly Kristi realized that the second shadow flitting across the tundra below was too big and moving too fast to be cast by a bird. Scanning the sky, she caught a glimpse of another plane, slightly above and to the left. It was banking straight for her.

She shoved the stick forward, sending her plane into a power dive, and waited, cringing on the edge of her seat for the sound of ripping metal. None came. As she leveled off, she spotted the intruder preparing to land on the water below.

Her heart began pounding in delayed reaction, and she sucked in a steadying breath. "All this empty sky, and he almost ran me down!" she cried hoarsely. The pilot must be a *cheechako*—a tenderfoot—to be flying around in that rich man's toy as though he owned the sky. She'd go after him to set him straight before he killed some poor unsuspecting soul.

Ahead of her, the blue-and-white craft bellied into the water and began taxiing toward the sandy beach. It wasn't a half-bad landing, she had to admit, but she'd show the greenhorn a thing or two about flying.

Buzzing over the other plane, Kristi brought her Cessna 180 down in front of it, skimming along the surface, spraying water behind. At the last moment, she cut the engine and nosed the floats into shore.

If her father had seen that hotshot stunt, he'd have grounded her for sure, she thought, shaking her head in disgust. But her lips curved into a satisfied smile as she gave the control column a quick pat. The old workhorse had done her proud.

Climbing out on the float, she jumped ashore and began tying up to a stunted willow bush.

Water lapped at her rubber-soled boots, heralding the arrival of the flying boat on the beach. Partly hidden by the willows, Kristi took inventory of the pilot as he flipped up the hatch and climbed out to sit on the wing—long legs enhanced by formfitting jeans, lean muscular body nicely packaged in a black leather flying jacket, curly chestnut hair that brushed the tops of his ears, and a tanned face that would be a perfect model for Prince Charming. Altogether, he was a handsome fly-boy, sexy enough to match his plane.

Devlin King sat on the wing, breathing in deep lungfuls of cool arctic air, wondering if he'd manage to get out of the north alive. This lake had almost claimed a second King! And it had been his own fault. He hadn't been expecting another plane up here in no-man's-land. If that white-haired bush pilot hadn't been flying the Cessna, he'd be shaking St. Peter's hand. He jumped down onto the sand, grateful to shake the sourdough's hand instead.

"That was some mighty fancy flying," Dev said, then stopped abruptly as the other pilot marched around the bush toward him.

The sourdough was a woman. A slender, fair-haired, blue-eyed beautiful woman. A woman who was so totally alive, she positively glowed. And he'd almost snuffed out her glow permanently, he thought, as his heart skipped, stalled, then began hammering erratically.

"I have a good mind to report you to the FAA," she said, coming to a stop a few feet from him. "Pilots like you shouldn't be allowed loose up here. You should be in the safe south with an air traffic controller to baby-sit you." She waved her hand as though trying to banish him back where he belonged. "Besides being a menace to everyone else, you're probably lost."

"Yes, ma'am, I'm lost." He moved closer, wanting to reach out and touch her, to reassure himself that she was real. He raised his hand, then realizing what he'd been about to do, shoved it through his hair instead. "Completely," he added hoarsely.

She held her ground, tilting her head up to glare at him. "You had the whole Alaskan sky, yet you nearly ran me down. Why weren't you watching where you were going?"

Dev barely heard her as he got lost in her clear blue eyes. They were the same blue as the myriad of lakes he'd flown over. A man could dive into them and remain forever.

Kristi waited for the stranger to defend himself, but he just kept looking at her with such a bemused expression on his face, she didn't have the heart to remain angry. His eyes were moss-green with laughter crinkles at the corners. And two grooves bracketed his wide mouth. He must have smiled for most of his thirty-odd years, Kristi thought, her own lips relaxing in a responsive smile. "Okay, maybe I was partly to blame, but I didn't expect anyone to be flying around . . ."

Dev gazed down at her intently, shutting out her words. Her thick white-gold hair hugged her shapely head like a cap. The tip of her elegant nose turned up just slightly. And her full red lips were made for kissing, not scolding, he decided.

His mind wandered as he thought about kissing her, wanting it so badly he could taste it, feel it in every part of his body.

Giving in to the urge, he took the final step that separated them, bowed his head, and silenced her with a kiss. His hands cupped her face gently as he savored her sweet lips. They softened in a surprised gasp, and he wanted to go on kissing her for an eternity. The moment passed and he felt her lips harden, her body stiffen. Releasing her, he stepped back, waiting for the slap he so richly deserved.

She stared at him, her eyes wide, then glanced over his shoulder and laughed—an infectious husky laugh that touched his senses. A laugh that made him want to curl up with her by a warm fire. A laugh definitely not in keeping with what he'd just done.

"You find my kiss amusing? I must be losing my touch." A coaxing grin tugged at the corner of his mouth. "Let me try again."

Shaking her head, she stepped aside. "You've got better things to do than kiss me, Romeo."

"Like what?"

She pointed toward the water. Turning, Dev saw the reason for her mirth. His plane was ten feet offshore and drifting toward the middle of the lake. With a yelp of surprise, he waded after it, then yelped again as the cold water ran down the insides of his cowboy boots.

"Yeow! It's freezing!"

"What did you expect? The ice just went out a few weeks ago." Her laughter flowed across the distance between them like a merrily bubbling stream.

He gauged the distance to the nose cowling. How could the plane have floated so far in such a short time? A ripple of wind caught the wing, pushing it farther out of reach, giving him the answer.

Turning, he sent her a beseeching smile. "How 'bout giving me a hand."

"You fly that big boy's toy, you look after it," she said, knowing that if he couldn't haul the plane ashore, she could rescue it with hers.

"Heartless woman. Just you wait until I get back. I expect you to warm me up."

Kristi stood on the bank, bemused. What did he mean by warm him up? He didn't plan on kissing her again. Or did he? The kiss had been so unexpected, she hadn't had time to be frightened before it was over. She might even enjoy another kiss.

What was she thinking? She'd be a fool to let this handsome green-eyed fly-boy kiss her again, or even get close.

In all the years she'd worked in the North, she'd never been afraid when a stranger flew into camp. Of course her father had usually been with her, but on many occasions he'd left her alone, confident she could look after herself.

And she had, except for that one time. . . .

With an impatient shake of her head, she buried the memory in the permafrost where it belonged and turned her attention to the stranger in the water. He might be a threat, but she had learned her lesson well.

"What's your name so I know what to put on your frozen corpse when I send it south?" she asked, dispelling her thoughts with banter.

"Devlin King," he said with a gasp as he edged deeper into the water. "My friends call me Dev."

Kristi only heard the Dev part but let it pass. The *cheechako* wasn't going to be around long enough for his last name to matter. "Where do I send you?" she asked, wondering why she continued to tease him. She was about as adept at making small talk as a moose was walking on bare ice.

"Houston."

"Figures." She laughed again as he took another short step, making no progress. "Why don't you rope it, cowboy?"

"I left my horse at home."

Bracing himself for the inevitable, Dev took two long strides. The frigid water swirled midthigh, sending icicles up his spine. Another lunge, and he caught the nose. Leaning back, he dug in his heels, stopping the plane's progress, then backed toward shore, pulling it with him.

He definitely has muscles, Kristi noted, admiring the way his broad shoulders filled out the worn bomber jacket and his wet jeans clung to his legs. She stepped forward to help, then stopped dead as she caught sight of the distinctive black, green, and gold flag on the plane's tail.

The logo for King Oil.

She closed her eyes tightly, trying to shut out the images of the oil-soaked nesting grounds near Cordova, the floundering swans, and of her father trapped in the twisted wreckage of his plane. Slowly she opened her eyes. The flag was still there.

So it had finally begun.

She'd been expecting the Baron, the head of King Oil, to react to the blistering letter she'd written him.

But why would he send such a greenhorn to confront her? Her stomach knotted as a possible answer struck her.

"What did you say your name was?"

"Devlin King."

"You're the Baron's son?" Kristi asked, realizing she didn't know his father's real name. People called him the Oil Baron, or the Baron of King Oil. She, however had called him many other names, none fit to print.

Dev heaved on the plane again. "Yep."

"Why don't you climb aboard and fly that boat out of here," she said, meaning it as an order.

"I'll be happy to as soon as I take care of some unfinished family business."

Kristi knew she was the "unfinished family business." The Baron must have taken seriously her threat to fight King Oil at every environmental hearing from now to doomsday. And well he should have. She had meant every word of it, and as soon as her father was fully recovered from the accident, he'd be out there leading the campaign to stop any future drilling by King Oil. And, as usual, she'd be working behind the scenes, providing him with the necessary ammunition.

They had opposed one of King Oil's applications, and although that hadn't turned out the way Kristi had hoped—mainly due to her ineptness—the Baron had probably decided it would be easier to discredit them than to face them at another hearing.

Kristi shivered as a tingle of apprehension climbed her spine. What if Devlin King did find something he could twist around and use against them? Three years of research would go down the drain. Not to mention the funding which they needed to make the final payment on the lodge. And thanks to the accident, the lodge had become more than a dream—it had become a necessity. It would be months before her father would walk again, and it was doubtful if he'd ever be able to do fieldwork.

Angrily, Kristi shook off the chill. Well just let Mr. Devlin King try. Their research was solid, and they had earned the respect of their colleagues years ago. It would be a short day in June before King Oil would ruin their reputation.

With one last heave, Dev skidded the nose of the plane up on the shore. Then grumbling something about insensitive women, he removed ropes and stakes from the cockpit and anchored the plane to the sandy beach.

Kristi watched him, trying to size him up, wondering why the Baron had sent Dev instead of his oldest son, Duke. She'd met Dev's brother at a hearing and had learned the hard way that Duke was a formidable opponent. However, she suspected Dev, with his sexy smile and potent charm, could be just as formidable. She knew how to handle Duke. Dev was another matter altogether.

"So, what are you doing here?" she asked sweetly, as Dev reached into the backseat of his plane, pulled out a navy duffel bag, and plopped it down on the sand.

Dev shivered. "Freezing to death."

Bending over, he quickly pulled off his boots and soggy socks, revealing long slim feet. Very blue feet, Kristi noted, smiling in amusement. It served him right. Abruptly her smile faded. The right foot was pitted with scars. He rubbed it across the top of the left, then dug his toes into the sand.

"It's August." Dev shivered again and worked his toes into the warm sand. "It's supposed to be summer."

"This is Alaska, not Texas. Best hightail it home where it's hotter than a crematorium."

He let his gaze roam over her, taking in first her faded jeans then her powder-blue turtle neck sweater. "And the cold isn't affecting you?"

Puzzled, Kristi glanced down at herself. To her horror she discovered that the cold had hardened her nipples. Had he noticed they were tenting her body-hugging sweater? Looking up, she saw the twinkle in his green eyes and the appreciative smile on his lips. He'd noticed all right.

"Do you always flirt so outrageously with every woman you meet?" she asked, disconcerted by his stare. How could he appear so sexy and so innocent at the same time? And why wasn't she taking offense?

He thumped his chest with a closed fist. "You wound me, ma'am. I'm really very harmless."

"Tell me another one. You look about as harmless as a polecat in a chicken coop."

Throwing back his head, he laughed, and to her amazement, Kristi found herself joining in. Why was she taking so much delight in this silly conversation? she wondered. True, he was the first person she'd seen in weeks. But he was one of the enemy, for heaven's sake. She wasn't *that* starved for company!

Hand on his belt buckle, he cocked his head to one side. "Well, ma'am, are you going to turn your back, or am I?"

"What are you talking about?"

"So you're one of those liberated women, are you?" He turned away. "Well, I'm the shy type," he said as he began shucking his wet jeans down his legs.

Mouth gaping in surprise, Kristi could only stand and watch. Tight blue cotton appeared first, then tanned muscular thighs, and finally powerful legs, covered with fine brown hair and goose bumps.

Kicking his feet free of the jeans, he shifted his hips to maintain his balance. Kristi's gaze followed the movement. She swallowed, trying to stifle the small sound in the base of her throat. Hearing it, he glanced over his shoulder and caught her staring. She gave a choked laugh.

"You find me funny?" he asked, his right brow arching.

Dressed as he was, in a bomber jacket and briefs, he should have looked ridiculous. He didn't. Ad men would kill to have him model their briefs. Speechless, she shook her head.

"Well, ma'am, I hate to curtail your enjoyment, but it's cold out here."

Pulling a pair of clean jeans out of the duffel bag, he stepped into them and hiked them up.

Indecent, decadent, dangerous, Kristi's mind warned. But her traitorous body quivered in warm response. Never before had the sight of a man's taut tush stirred her.

He turned around, and Kristi couldn't help but admire the front view too. The soft denim hugged him like kid leather. Realizing she was staring again, she raised her gaze to his face, then blushed as his knowing smile made it very plain she'd been caught in the act.

An impish gleam danced in his eyes as he moved toward her. She retreated a step, then stopped. Her Sitka boots would hold their own against his bare feet. Her knees didn't believe her—they trembled. Pressing them together, she straightened her shoulders and made the most of her five feet seven. Even barefoot he topped her by six inches.

"Just what are you doing up here anyway?" she asked again, trying to restore some semblance of order to her mind. Hopefully, her body would follow suit.

Dev gazed down at her, thinking she looked like a bantam rooster, trying to act cocky while pretending that she wasn't the least bit aware of him. But she was definitely aware of him—the glow in her eyes told him so, as did her quivering lips—and he wondered what she would do if he kissed her again. Probably sock him, he thought. Most women he knew would've been hightailing it for home.

He took another step forward, then stopped as he saw the flicker of fear in her eyes. Suddenly aware of how vulnerable she was, he backed off and bent over to pick up his boots. It certainly hadn't been his intention to frighten her . . . or to come on too strong. What in heaven's name was she doing there, anyway? It was no place for a woman. Especially a woman alone.

He straightened and frowned at her in concern. "Why are *you* flying around this barren wasteland?" he asked, holding the boots upside down to drain the water.

"I was counting birds," she said huskily, then took a deep breath and cleared her throat. "Mainly Tundra Swans. You probably know them as whistling swans. Anyway, they're the ones you frightened when you landed.

"I wondered what they were. There's a pair on almost every lake north of the Brooks Range." Grimacing, he shook the last drops of water out of the boots then hung them upside down over the willows. "But isn't it dangerous to be working alone?"

"I don't work alone, I work with my father," Kristi said, not feeling the least bit guilty about telling a white lie, especially when Dev kept avoiding her question. When was he going to admit that he knew about the oil spill and her father's accident? And how long was she going to let him get away with it before she confronted him?

No, she wouldn't confront him, she decided. She'd wait until he told her the real reason why he'd come north. More than likely she'd have to wait until hell froze over or the permafrost melted, but she'd wait.

"Well, thank goodness you're not out here all by yourself," Dev said, wondering what there was about this lady that made him feel protective one minute, then disappointed the next because he had no reason to protect her. The near miss in the plane must have addled his brain.

No doubt about it, his brain was definitely addled, he decided after further reflection. None of his acquaintances would ever believe that he had talked to a woman for half an hour, had even kissed her, and he didn't even know who she was.

He shook his head in bemusement, then smiled at her. "I just realized I don't know your name."

The smile was so wide, it creased his cheeks and crinkled the corners of his eyes. And confirmed Kristi's suspicion. Devlin King made his way through life with his good looks and charm—a very potent mixture.

"Kristen Bjornson," she answered. Then warming in spite of herself, she added, "Kristi."

"Kristi. I like it."

The soft husky way he said her name sent a tingle through her. It was almost as though he had whispered it in her ear.

"Bjornson." He rubbed his jaw thoughtfully. "I've heard the name before."

You bet your boots you have, Kristi thought, her senses reeling with renewed wariness and unwanted awareness of him. Devlin King was a dangerous man in more ways than one. Well, he wasn't going to breech *her* defenses with his charm.

Clamping her hands on her hips, she glared up at him. "We haven't met."

"I know. Believe me, I would've remembered meeting you." He smiled again. "And where do you call home?"

"Cordova." The word conjured up vivid images of black oil, dying swans, and mangled flesh and bones, and suddenly Kristi was sick and tired of the sparring game. "You still haven't told me why you're here," she said abruptly.

His smile faded as he looked down at his feet, then up at her. "I came to a place a marker on my grandfather's grave."

Two

Kristi stared at Dev, her jaw slack. She snapped it shut decisively. Her mouth had been open far too much for one day.

"There's no grave around here." She had to hand it to him, though. It was a marvelous excuse to snoop around her turf in the hopes he could find something to use against her.

With a nod of his head, Dev strode toward his plane. Kristi followed, intrigued despite her reservations. Reaching into the cockpit, he removed an aeronautical chart and spread it out on the wing. "Is this where we are?" he asked, pointing out a lake.

Kristi leaned forward, catching the scent of leather mixed with his spicy after-shave. She inhaled slowly, liking the way it filled her nostrils, realizing for the first time in her life just how good a man could smell. This is ridiculous, she told herself. Just because she hadn't seen a man for two months was no reason to go all mushy over the first one who came along.

Reining in her thoughts, she focused her attention on the chart. "Yes," she said, after getting her bearings.

"I thought so. If my information is correct, the King's grave—grandfather's grave—should be right over there." He pointed toward the high rocky over-look at the end of the lake. "I was trying to locate it when I almost hit you. By the way, I don't think I've apologized yet, Kristi," he said, his eyes and smile reflecting his concern.

She ignored his apology but couldn't ignore his smile. It made her feel warm and somehow cher-ished. "What was your grandfather doing here?"

"Flying home from the north shore. He got caught in an early snowstorm and crashed. When they found the plane two years later, the Duchess—sorry, I mean my grandmother—asked them to bury his remains on top of the hill." He shuddered, thinking how close he had come to joining his grandfather in an unmarked grave. Along with Kristi. Heaven help him, he had almost killed her. Again he had the overwhelming urge to take her in his arms but turned away instead, not trusting himself to be content with just holding her.

"Likely story," Kristi said, her suspicion rekindled. For a moment there, when she had looked into his eyes, she had almost believed him, but then he'd turned his back on her. "I've flown over here hun-dreds of times, and I haven't seen any wreckage."

Dev slowly replaced the chart in the plane before facing her again. "King Oil hauled it out. They didn't want to clutter up the landscape."

"Tell me another one," Kristi scoffed, knowing from recent experience just how little regard King Oil had for the environment. "Like the real reason you're here."

"It *is* the real reason." Dev sighed. He couldn't blame her for being skeptical. It did sound pretty farfetched. "If you don't believe me, come along and see for yourself."

"You're not going up there—"

"Oh, but I am."

"On bare feet?"

Dev stared down at his feet, then looked up with a

lopsided smile on his lips. "You wouldn't happen to have an extra pair of boots with you?" he asked hopefully.

The smile tugged at something deep inside, and Kristi shook her head regretfully. "Sorry, not with me, but I could probably scrounge up a pair of hipwaders at—" What in heaven's name was she thinking about? Next she'd be inviting him back to camp.

With a sigh of resignation, Dev climbed into his plane and fished around in the backseat. Opening the bag of souvenirs he'd purchased in Fairbanks, he removed a well-wrapped package, then collected his cameras and sat in the passenger's seat.

He hesitated a moment, debating whether he should put the pendant with the rest of the souvenirs, but after a quick pat of the breast pocket of his bomber jacket, he decided to leave it where it was. It was safe there. Besides, it felt right at home, nestled next to his heart.

The pendant would suit Kristi, he thought, then shook his head at his foolishness. Just because a piece of walrus-tusk ivory had almost flown off the display case into his pocket didn't mean he had to give it to the first woman he met.

"Kristi, would you mind giving me a hand unloading this stuff?" he called out, still thinking that the pendant would suit her.

She came closer, and Dev passed things down to her. Package in hand, he vaulted out of the plane, landing on feet that smarted sharply in protest. He hopped up and down, swearing softly, then flashed Kristi an apologetic grin. The grin faded as he held the package at arm's length and wrinkled his nose in anticipation. He did not want to open it, not even a crack. Taking a final deep breath of pure air, he tore away the brown paper, revealing a pair of beaded moccasins.

"Whooee, those are rank," Kristi said, backing

away quickly as the arid smell of smoked leather assaulted her nostrils.

He dropped the moccasins to the ground and stared at them in disgust. "I sure hadn't planned on wearing them."

"Then why buy them?" she asked, laughing at the woeful expression on his face.

"A present for my present-giving brother, Dare," he said as he dug a pair of socks out of the duffel bag and pulled them on. He'd been tempted to buy a pair for Duke and his father, too, but didn't think they'd appreciate the joke. Not that it mattered. He wasn't even on speaking terms with them.

Kristi studied Dev more carefully. He was gazing at his feet as though he had lost something precious, and she gripped the strap of the camera he'd handed her tightly so she wouldn't give in to the temptation to reach out and touch him. "Well, hurry up and put them on and take these things from me," she said lightly. "I want to hold my nose."

He flashed her a sheepish grin as he slipped into the oversize moccasins, then moved closer and began draping straps over his shoulder. "Are you coming?"

"You bet I am," she said, reaching for the video camera that dangled precariously from his arm. "Here, I'll carry this."

"Thanks."

The strap tangled around Dev's wrist and as he shook it free, his hand brushed her breast and lingered an instant too long. Kristi caught her breath as her nipples responded, and her blue eyes, full of the new awareness, sought his.

Slowly, he lowered his hand. "Sorry about that," he said, knowing he lied. He wasn't one bit sorry. Startled, perhaps, that Kristi was so soft, because she didn't carry an extra ounce of flesh on her sleek limbs.

Kristi continued to stare at him, heart racing, for

another breathless second, then slung the camera over her shoulder and strode purposefully along the beach. He kept pace, and she knew without looking at him that he was smiling down at her.

"Why all the cameras?" she asked, hoping she didn't sound as flustered as she felt.

She was so cute when she was flustered, Dev thought. He considered teasing her a little more, just to see if he could get a rise out of her, then decided against it. Best stick to business. He didn't have time to hang around, no matter how tempting it was to get to know this intriguing woman better.

"I want to take pictures of the King's gravesite for my grandmother," he explained, a warm feeling settling in the region of his heart as he suddenly realized that Kristi reminded him of his grandmother. "The Dutchess would've insisted on coming along if I'd told her where I was going. But my father would've objected, and I didn't want to cause a row."

His voice sounded so full of love that for a moment Kristi wondered if he might be telling the truth.

"Where's the marker?" she asked, reminding herself that she couldn't let down her guard for an instant, especially with this smooth-talking stranger.

"In the plane."

"Why aren't you bringing it with you?"

"I'm not that crazy. I want to know the exact location of the grave before I lug it one inch."

"Well, let's brave the permafrost and go find this grave," she said, stepping off the sand into the tundra. Silver-green reindeer moss crunched underfoot. It *would* have to be dry here, she noted in wry amusement. In most places the tundra was so spongy, Dev's feet would have been soaked in no time.

Realizing he wasn't following, she turned to wait for him. He was watching her, a puzzled expression on his face. "You really don't believe there is a grave, do you?" he asked, as he approached her.

"No." She shifted her weight from foot to foot.

"Then why are you coming along?"

"Simple. To make sure you don't harm my birds."

His lips twitched. "My, my, aren't you being possessive now. My birds."

"Well, someone has to protect them from people like you," she said, the memory of what had happened near Cordova that spring fueling her anger. Thanks to the carelessness of one of King Oil's employees, a prime nesting ground for the trumpeter swans had been destroyed. And her father had almost died trying to rescue the poor birds. If she had her way, the culprit would be tarred and feathered, along with his employers—including Devlin King.

"People like me?"

"All your family has ever been concerned about is making money. You don't care what happens to the land or the wildlife in the process."

Dev gazed at her in admiration, ignoring the telling but unfortunately true comments she'd made about his family. Lord, but he liked her style. Blue eyes glowing with conviction, she was a Viking queen ready to wage war for her beliefs. She was definitely someone he'd want on his side when it came to fighting issues—a woman after his own heart. No, he did not want her by his side, he reminded himself. Once was enough. Never again would he allow a woman like Kristi close to his heart.

"You really *love* the birds, don't you?" he asked, testing the waters although he already knew the answer.

"You bet. And I'm going to do my damnedest to make sure no one will ever harm them or their nesting grounds again."

Her enthusiasm brought a warm smile to his lips. "I intend them no harm."

During the space of two wingbeats, Kristi got lost

in his smile, then forced herself to remember Dev was a *King*. "Tell that to the birds," she said.

"All I ask is that you reserve judgment until we find the grave," he said softly.

She studied him intently for a moment, before waving her hand toward the outcrop of rocks. "Lead on, *Cheechako*. Show me this grave."

In silence they began climbing the hill. Midstride, Dev noticed he was about to step on some purple flowers. He managed to miss the first patch but realized it would be impossible to avoid them all. The moss-covered rocks were carpeted with tiny pink, blue, and purple blossoms—a rock garden only nature could create.

"I knew flowers grew up here, but there're so many."

Kristi glanced at him, then smiled at the look of amazement on his face. "This is the land of igloos and polar bears, right?"

"And unexpected beauty." His gaze swept slowly over her. "I'd sure hate to spoil it."

A shiver of expectancy touched her spine as she wondered if he was also talking about her. Careful, careful, she warned herself. The very fact he'd even noticed the flowers surprised her. And his concern about stepping on them made him all the more endearing and therefore extremely dangerous to her.

Suddenly impatient to end this farce, she began the final assault on the hill. At the top, she turned to watch him climb the last few feet. "Now where is that grave?"

As he came abreast, his gaze focused on a point beyond her left shoulder. The tender expression in his eyes stopped her next words cold. Swinging around, she saw the pile of rocks. They had obviously been placed there by man, not nature.

"It *is* a grave!"

"Yeah."

Remembering her recent disparaging remarks,

Kristi felt ashamed. "I'm sorry, Dev. I just didn't believe you."

"He was so good to me," Dev said huskily. "When he died, I not only lost a grandfather, but also the best companion I ever had. He used to—" His voice choked to a halt, and he turned abruptly to look down at the lake.

Kristi stood beside him in silence, wishing there was something she could say. But she'd said more than enough already. Instead, she studied the grave-site, giving Dev a moment of privacy.

Finally he pivoted on his heel and moved slowly toward the grave.

"Wait!" she whispered urgently, catching his arm to hold him back.

"But I want to find a place for the marker."

"You can't put up a marker. Not now."

Dev stared at her in bewilderment. "What are you talking about?"

"Look." Kristi pointed toward the far end of the pile of stones. "A snowy owl is nesting right next to the grave."

After a moment Dev spotted the white-and-brown mound of feathers crouched in a hollow depression in the tundra. As he watched, the owl's head swiveled around and lemon-yellow eyes stared at him dreamily.

Squeezing Dev's arm, Kristi brought his attention to the scruffy ball of white fluff sitting in a patch of pink flowers a short distance away.

"An ookpik!" Dev whispered in delight. He remembered when white pom-pom replicas of the owlet had been the rage and recalled his grandmother's pleasure when he'd given her one for her birthday.

"There's only one chick," Kristi said regretfully. "What a shame. Normally she lays about eight eggs."

Intrigued, he stepped forward for a better view but halted as Kristi tightened her grip on his arm.

"What are you trying to do, frighten the poor thing?" she asked softly.

"I sure don't want to disturb her, but how'n the devil am I going to place the marker?"

Dismayed to discover she was still gripping his arm, Kristi released it quickly and shoved her hand into the back pocket of her jeans. "Your father can send someone out to erect it after the birds have left. Or I'll do it for you," she offered.

Dev smiled down at Kristi in gratitude. "Thanks, but I have to do this myself. Call it a mission or whatever, but that's the way it has to be."

Again Kristi felt the heart warming effect of his smile, and again she forced herself to ignore it. "Why is it so important that you put up the marker?"

"It's something I want to do for my grandmother," he said quietly. The Duchess had been the only member of the family who had stood by him these past three years. Sure Dare had continued to send his corny gifts, and he knew that his mother loved him. But Madre's loyalty lay with her husband, and there had been nothing but silence from his father, the Baron. Cold, hard, unrelenting silence. Knowing how his father had felt about the King's yearly trips to Alaska, he doubted if erecting the marker would soften the silence, but it was still something he wanted to do. For his grandmother, for the family, for himself.

"Well if you want to put up the marker, you'll have to hang around until after the owlet has fledged," Kristi said, breaking into his thoughts.

"When will that be?"

"A week. Maybe two."

Dev stared at Kristi in dismay. "I can't wait two weeks."

"What's so pressing that you have to rush home?"

"An important engagement," he said, offering no further explanation. The president was expecting him for dinner a week from Friday, but that wasn't something he could casually tell Kristi. And there was the commission he'd just been appointed to chair. The commission concerning the most important cause he'd ever taken on. Not only because it could affect his chances of becoming a senator, but because it could either protect or destroy one of the most ecologically important regions in the world—the wetlands along the Gulf coast.

"With a beautiful woman who doesn't like to be kept waiting, I bet," Kristi said, aware that his thoughts were far away. Not that it mattered one pinfeather to her, how many beautiful women this sexy man had back home, she told herself.

"You think I'm a spoiled playboy, don't you?"

"If the shoe fits."

He glanced down at the moccasins. They were too large—as had been all the other family shoes he'd tried to wear until he'd finally taken a stand. The stand had won him a seat in Congress but had cost him his family. Usually he was too busy to count the cost, but occasionally—like now—the loneliness caught up with him, making him wonder if it had been worth it.

Raising his head, he looked at Kristi. She was beside him, watching him intently, her hair glowing in the sunlight. Without warning, a wave of awareness washed through Dev, filling him with a warm certainty that shook him to the core. With Kristi by his side, he'd never have to stand alone.

But Kristi would never stay by his side; she had her own cause—her birds—he reminded himself, feeling doubly desperate to leave. If he hung around for long, he might find himself falling in love with her. And he'd been down that road once before. "Are you sure I couldn't put up the marker?" he asked abruptly. "After all, it's only one bird."

She frowned her disapproval. "Only one bird! If everyone had your attitude, there wouldn't be one, single, solitary bird left on this earth."

Dev gave her a sheepish look. For a moment there,

his unwanted attraction toward Kristi had scrambled his brain so badly, he'd forgotten everything—even the commission he was chairing and the millions of birds he hoped to protect. "I didn't mean it that way," he said.

"Are you sure you just came up here to put a marker on the grave and nothing more?" she asked, his apology doing nothing to alleviate her suspicion.

He nodded at the pile of stones. "There's the grave."

Kristi gave Dev a skeptical glance, wondering whether to believe his words or the guilty expression on his face. The grave was certainly real, but so was the letter she'd written to his father. She'd still bet her last dime that the Baron had sent his son up there on a sabotage mission, using the grave as a cover.

A smile touched Kristi's lips as a germ of an idea flitted through her brain. She repressed the smile, but let the idea have full rein. Maybe, just maybe, she could turn the tables on the high-and-mighty Baron. It would serve him right if she could convert one of his sons into an environmentalist and have the opposition come from within his own camp. Considering the history of King Oil and anyone connected with it, she doubted she could succeed, but she'd give it her best shot. However, she'd have to be careful not to tip her hand too soon.

As the silence stretched between them, Kristi noticed Dev's eyes grow speculative. Quickly she lowered her head, hoping he hadn't read her thoughts.

Dev studied her carefully, wondering how far he could push this determined young woman. He didn't have time to wait around for a bird to fly. In fact he shouldn't be there at all. He should be back in Washington, lobbying his fellow congressmen for support. It was still questionable whether or not his commission would even get off the ground.

Certainly he could ignore Kristi's wishes and put

up the marker; however, she already held the King family in contempt. Maybe he could negotiate a compromise . . . one that would allow him to accomplish his mission without creating any more bad feelings and be on his way back to Washington within twenty-four hours. After all, he was known on the Hill as the charming congressman from Texas. It was time to put his so-called charm to use.

"This is Sunday, isn't it?" She nodded. "Well I guess I can hang around for a few days, maybe even a week," he said, flashing her an engaging smile. It wouldn't do to let her guess just how soon he wanted to leave.

"I can't promise the owlet will fly by then," Kristi warned, trying to ignore his smile.

"I'll take the chance," Dev said, wondering how he was going to wrangle an invitation to stay with Kristi. He couldn't coax her into changing her mind if he was in Fairbanks. And her father would be in camp, so there'd be nothing improper about him staying there. Maybe Bjornson would be more reasonable than his daughter and would even help him convince Kristi to let him erect the marker on the King's grave.

Turning, he slowly surveyed the flat terrain, trying to collect his thoughts. The hill was the only high spot for miles, and the tundra stretched forever, decked out in gold and brown and splashes of vivid red. Below him the calm lake sparkled like a jewel, and hundreds of other jewels shimmered south to the shadowy mountains and north to the top of the world. No wonder the King had returned to Alaska year after year.

Kristi watched the expressions chase across Dev's handsome face. He was such an easygoing man, but there was a core of hardness under his charm.

"It's beautiful," he said in awe.

She smiled, pleased he was falling under the spell of the North. That was the first step in converting him. "It has a beauty all its own, one that grows on you."

"I might as well pitch my tent down by the lake and wait right here," he said, guessing she would refuse if he came right out and asked to stay with her.

Kristi studied Dev through veiled lashes, wondering if she dared invite him back to camp. The last time a stranger had stayed with her she'd make an absolute fool of herself, but she was no longer that shy naive girl. She knew all about men and their charms. And it would be worth the risk if she could convert Dev.

"You'd better fly on to Barrow," she said slyly, knowing it wouldn't do to appear too anxious. "Or better yet, return to Fairbanks. You can find more suitable accommodations there—and night spots."

"Your suggestion is tempting, but I'm not here to hit the night spots and I don't have time to waste. The minute the little one flies, I do too."

"Well, I'm not about to leave you here."

He pulled a sad face. "So, you don't trust me alone with the birds?"

"You got it. You'd best come stay with me so I can keep an eye on you."

"Well, thank you, ma'am, for your kind invitation, even though you're only asking me so you can protect your birds," he said, bending over to pick up his camera equipment. He straightened, smiling, and Kristi abruptly turned her back and started down the hill. Dev caught up with her in three long strides, and they walked in silence to the beach.

What was she thinking of Kristi wondered, asking this stranger to stay with her? She probably needed protection from Dev more than the birds did. Every time he smiled, she felt like melting. What would she do if he really turned on the charm?

"We'll head for camp," Kristi said, then took a deep breath, wishing she didn't sound as if she'd just run the Iditarod. "Are you on a flight plan?"

"Ummhmm," he said, stopping at the bush to retrieve his jeans and boots and pile them on top of his cameras.

"Well, radio in and tell them you're staying with me." She lifted the video camera into the passenger seat of his plane, then turned in time to catch the boots sliding earthward. "That way, if anyone comes looking for you, the moccasin telegraph can tell them where to find you," she said as she tossed his boots into the plane and brushed off her hands.

A lopsided smile tugged at the corner of his mouth. "Moccasin telegraph?"

Distracted by the smile and the hummingbird which began hovering below her heart, Kristi stuttered an explanation. "It's . . . it's hard to explain how it works . . . but somehow we manage to keep track of each other. We know where everyone is camped and what they are doing and where they are going and . . ." She gave a little shrug.

"And where are *we* going?"

"To another lake a few miles from here. Do you think you can follow without running into me?"

His smile broadened. "I can follow you to the ends of the world."

This time Kristi's heart did a loop-de-loop. "Oh, heavens! Spare me." And thank heavens Rex was in camp, she thought, as she climbed into her plane. At the rate she was going, she would definitely need his protection.

Three

Dev sat motionless on the wing of his plane and watched a sharp-faced gray-and-white husky bound forward to greet Kristi, who had just finished tying her floats to a tiedown ring.

"Hello, boy. Miss me?" she asked, scratching the dog behind the ears while he licked her tanned cheek. Kristi straightened to smile at Dev as he slid to the ground and began pounding a stake into the sand. "Meet Rex, my guard dog."

Dev ignored the dog, which was sniffing at his moccasins, and ran a rope from the stake to the wing of his plane. "Rex? That's Latin for king, isn't it?"

"Yes."

"I don't like dogs, and I'm sharing a name with one!"

Kristi snapped her fingers and summoned Rex to her side. "I wondered how you'd react to that," she said, disappointed that Dev didn't like dogs. In her book any person worth his salt had to like—if not love—dogs. She had another good reason to distrust Devlin King.

"Just tell him to keep his distance," he muttered, turning to survey the camp. One orange tent sat on a gravel bar a few yards up from the lake. One shapely pair of jeans hung on the guide rope. Nearby sat a tarped lean-to which contained a table, one campstool, and a couple of wooden crates, but no signs of another person. He turned back to look at Kristi with a puzzled frown. "I thought you said you were working with your father. Where is he?"

Kristi ducked her head in embarrassment, realizing that she had just been caught in her lie. Damn. Why hadn't she thought of it earlier when she'd been tricking him into coming back to camp?

"He's in the hospital, recovering from an accident," she told Dev, daring him to make something of it.

Dev's frown deepened as he wondered by he was suddenly feeling concerned about Kristi's safety. He hadn't felt this way about a woman since Brenda—who'd at first lovingly called him a throwback to the cowboys of the old West, but later had protested that he was stifling her. "You mean you're out here all alone?"

"Yes."

"And you invited me, a total stranger, into your camp!" Dev shook his head in disbelief.

"I'm perfectly capable of looking after myself. Besides, I'm not alone. I have Rex."

"And now another King to protect you," he said, silently admitting that the possibility of Kristi wanting or needing his protection was remote. She was one self-sufficient lady, all right, but . . . "How can you stand not talking to someone for days on end?"

"Oh, I talk all the time," she said with a slight laugh. "To Rex and my birds. I'm not very good with people. I can manage to hold up my end of the conversation on a one-to-one basis, but put me in front of a crowd, and I clam up completely."

He smiled at her gently, realizing that under her bossy, brash exterior Kristi was basically shy. He'd have to treat her carefully or she'd go into hiding. "But don't you get lonely?" he asked softly. "Crave for human contact?"

"No," she said, then repeated in a firmer voice. "No."

Dev was tempted to probe into why she'd hesitated, then thought better of it. "Where do you want me to pitch my tent?"

She pointed. "Right next to mine."

"What? I thought you'd at least make me camp on the other side of the lake."

"I'm very tempted. But the land is so fragile, I try to keep my impact down to a minimum."

"Good plan. I'll share your tent. That way I won't impact the land at all."

"Nice try, *Cheechako,* but Rex already sleeps at the foot of my bedroll." He looked so dejected that Kristi laughed, shaking her head. What an outrageous flirt. She could just imagine the impact he'd have on her if she took him seriously. "Do you need any help with your tent?" she asked sweetly.

"You really think I'm a tenderfoot, don't you?"

She glanced pointedly at his moccasins. "I *know* you're a tenderfoot."

"You're right," he said, deciding to play along with her. She'd be more inclined to let him stay if she thought she had the upper hand. "I'll holler if I need help."

Sitting on her campstool in the opening of the camp kitchen-cum-office, Kristi found it difficult to keep her attention focused on her daily logbook. Her gaze kept wandering to the handsome stranger. He may not have known much about tents, but he did know how to read and follow directions. And the way he moved, so confidently, so gracefully, despite the oversize moccasins, made it even more difficult to keep her eyes off him.

It was just because she was happy to have someone around camp for a change, she told herself sternly. She hadn't realized how much she missed human company until Dev had asked if she was lonely. In the past her father had been there to share the long evenings, and she hadn't given much thought to how she'd feel when she began working alone. How would she survive days, weeks, even months of not having another living soul—except Rex—to talk to? Other field biologists managed, but could she? And did she really want to?

But it was the life she'd chosen, she reminded herself sternly. Once she'd dreamed of sharing this life with her husband, and for a short while six summers earlier, she'd thought she'd found him. But Fergus McIntyre had only been interested in stealing her research—and in taking anything else she'd been willing to give—not spending his life in the frozen North.

Now another stranger had come to camp, and, sure as shooting, he was intent on getting something from her—either information he could use against her, or her promise not to oppose King Oil at future environmental hearings.

With wary eyes she watched as he hung his wet jeans beside hers, then returned to the plane. After propping his boots over the low willows at the edge of the lake, he began hauling gear out—a duffel bag, a bulging plastic bag of gift-wrapped packages, a sleeping bag and a—

"What are you doing with a harpoon, of all things?" she called out as he approached.

Dev paused in front of the kitchen. "I went into a shop in Fairbanks and kinda got carried away. Before I left I'd bought gifts for everyone and this for myself." He hefted the barbed spear in his hand, pleased with its strength and balance. "I used to throw javelin in college."

"No football?" Kristi asked, her gaze lingering on his broad shoulders.

"You think I'm crazy! Those college jocks were bigger and meaner than me. Besides, I can't stand pain." His confident grin made a lie of the statement."

Still hefting the harpoon, Dev continued toward his tent. Kristi stared after him. Muscle-bound men had never turned her on, but Dev, in those jeans, was another matter altogether.

Horrified at the wayward course of her thoughts, Kristi forced her eyes back to the tally book. The numbers were blurred. With a sigh of resignation she gave up trying to make sense of them and patted Rex instead.

On his next trip from the lake Dev stopped again and held up two paper bags. "I'm afraid I wasn't thinking earlier. This is all the food I have, except for some freeze-dried stuff in the emergency kit."

Rising to her feet, Kristi walked out of the tent, Rex at her heels. "I imagine we'll survive without it." Her nose caught a tantalizing odor. "Smells good."

He offered her the white bag with the name of a Fairbanks bakery written on the side. "Doughnuts."

It was the other bag that interested Kristi. She took it from him eagerly.

Opening the bag, she breathed in the aroma with a wide smile on her lips. "Hmmm. You're forgiven."

"You like oranges?"

"Right about now I'd trade my soul for an orange. They're more precious than gold, even in Fairbanks, and I haven't been there for weeks."

"I wish I'd filled the plane. We grow them back home."

Kristi couldn't imagine living in a place where you could pick oranges off the trees. It was her idea of heaven.

"If you haven't been in town for weeks, how do keep enough supplies on hand?" Dev asked, looking around curiously.

"Come." Together they strolled across the campsite toward a twenty feet high hummock, with Rex trotting behind his mistress. Lifting a wooden door, she revealed a hole dug in the side of the mount. "Voila. Instant refrigeration."

"What is it?"

"A pingo. A frost heave. We're sitting on permafrost, you know. That's why there are so many lakes in the tundra. The snow melts but the water has nowhere to go." Removing one of the tin boxes, she opened it and placed the tempting oranges inside. Given half a chance, she'd eat the whole bag. "I'm trying to keep the odors down. Don't want to attract bears or wolves."

"Are there wolves around here?"

"A few. But they usually don't bother people unless they're starving or have gone mad."

He shivered despite the warmth of his jacket. "Well, that's one member of the dog family I definitely don't want to meet."

Kristi dropped the door on the food cache. "Since you didn't bring a big thick steak, we'd better go catch supper. You can fish, can't you, Tenderfoot?"

"Can I fish? Hey, you're talking to a man who was raised on the Gulf Coast." He'd been fishing the sum total of once in his life and had spent most of the time puking his guts over the side. But hell, he could fake it.

"Bring the doughnuts," she called over her shoulder as she headed toward the aviation fuel barrels at the edge of the lake.

Bag in hand, Dev followed slowly, watching her stride across the tundra. What a fascinating woman, this Kristi Bjornson, he thought. She was right at home in this barren land but looked as though she'd be equally at home on the runway of a fashion-design house. Even the heavy boots did nothing to detract from her long-legged graceful walk. Her waist was so tiny, he could easily span it with his hands. And her breasts . . . They were too large for a model's, but they suited him just fine.

Hold your horses! he told himself. Kristi Bjornson

was strictly off-limits. Never again was he going to get involved with a crusader, and Kristi was a crusader if he'd ever seen one. He needed someone who would stand by him, not go off on her own crusade.

Reaching her side, he flashed her a beguiling smile and hoped she couldn't read his thoughts.

"We'll use the canoe," she said, giving him a puzzled look. Removing two fishing rods and a tackle box from the top of the barrels, she placed them in the bottom of the green Fiberglas canoe and, with one deft twist of her body, floated it in the shallow water. "Climb in first and let me push you out."

A very *bossy* crusader, Dev thought as he scrambled into the canoe and moved gingerly to kneel in the bow. The canoe wobbled as Rex bounded in and settled down in the middle.

Dev glanced over his shoulder at the dog, which was leaning forward to sniff the bag of doughnuts. "You're taking him along?"

"He loves fishing."

Giving the canoe a shove, Kristi hopped nimbly aboard. The canoe rocked slightly, and Dev braced his hands on either side of the gunnel, shuddering at the thought of falling into the bone-chilling water.

"Lord preserve me. This thing's unstable enough without a dog."

"We've never had a problem before, so if anything happens, we'll know who to blame, won't we, Rex?"

The dog thumped his tail and barked sharply, making Dev jump and Kristi laugh. With a strong pull of her paddle, she sent the canoe away from shore. Dev picked up the other paddle and dipped it in the water. Not that he'd be much help, he thought ruefully. He couldn't remember the last time he'd paddled a canoe. After a few strokes he got the hang of it and began looking around with interest. Up ahead a loon dove gracefully into the water. A quacking duck flew over and landed in a patch of bulrushes next to the shore. The silence was broken only by the dip of the paddles and birdcalls.

Then Kristi's paddle rattled as she laid it in the bottom of the canoe. "This should do. Why don't you turn around and sit while we fish?"

"Turn around. She wants me to turn around," he grumbled, moving cautiously to do her bidding. By the time he was seated, Kristi had the hook on his line.

"Just to prove I trust you, you can use my father's rod." She passed it to him over the top of Rex's head. "However, let me warn you, if it goes overboard, you're going after it."

He took a good hold on the rod. "Warning noted," he muttered, wishing he hadn't spent most of his life in the city—although his time there had served him well. He'd been involved in one cause after another since he was sixteen, and he'd learned the best way to be effective was to be close to the decisionmakers, the lawmakers. His father had disagreed, maintaining that a man couldn't shoot the bull until he'd gotten his hands dirty shoveling it.

Well, he was about to get his hands dirty now, Dev thought. He watched Kristi make her first cast—expertly, he noted. Was there nothing Kristi couldn't do? He snaked out his line. The lure tumbled into the water a few feet from the canoe. Giving Kristi a lopsided grin, he reeled in the lure and tried again.

Kristi pressed her lips together to keep from returning the smile, then asked the question that had been niggling at the corner of her mind for hours. "When did your grandfather die?"

"Twenty years ago. I was ten at the time. For two years I kept hoping the King would turn up and tell me another fabulous story about his adventures in the North. He was my hero."

Kristi's heart softened as she thought about him as that boy. No wonder Dev had been so shaken when he'd seen the grave. She could imagine how devastated he must have been when he'd learned of his grandfather's death. "Why hasn't anyone put up a marker before now?" she asked softly.

Dev gave a short laugh as he made another cast. "Because my father has never forgiven the King for leaving his mother to fly north year after year."

"I can see where that might be a problem," Kristi said, thoughtfully. Her work meant she had to spend the summers in the arctic, and for that reason she'd never become seriously involved with a man. "Your grandmother must have been a very understanding wife to let him go."

"The Duchess used to tease him that he loved Alaska more than he loved her." Dev stared into the water, remembering how the words had returned to haunt him the day he'd learned that Brenda had loved something—not someone—more than him.

Looking up, he discovered that Kristi was watching him, and he smiled an apology for mentally drifting away from their conversation. "And I also remember the King saying he was fortunate to be blessed with a loving wife, because Alaska was a demanding mistress."

"I know what he means," she said softly. "I feel the same way."

"You really love the North, don't you?"

"I've lived here all my life. I like the excitement, the challenge the . . . I don't know . . . the feeling of being close to nature. I can't think of any other place I'd rather live."

Dev smiled at her enthusiasm, then sobered thoughtfully. "Have you ever considered moving south?"

"Why would I? Everything I want is here. My father, my work, my—" She broke off as a fish hit her hook.

Reeling in his line, Dev watched in admiration at the way Kristi played the fish. Lips pressed in determination, she wound in the slack, then dipped the rod to gain more leverage and wound again. The movement of her rounded breasts against her sweater captured his attention, distracting him from the main action. Mesmerized by the bewitching sight, and pleasantly aware of what it was doing to his own body, he was disappointed when she finally landed the fish. Pliers in hand, she gently removed the hook, then slipped the fish back into the water.

Dev shook his head in disbelief. "You let it go?"

"It's just a jack."

"Lady, you're crazy! That was the nicest fish I've ever seen."

"We're after arctic char."

"A fish is a fish."

Wiggling her nose at him, she made another cast. Still shaking his head, he followed suit.

"So tell me about your family," she said after the next cast, deciding now was a golden opportunity to learn more about the opposition—if Dev was willing to talk. "You refer to them as the King, the Duchess, the Baron, the Duke. Kind of an overkill isn't it?"

He chuckled softly, pleased that his last cast had finally matched hers. "The Duchess once sang for royalty and thought King was a more fitting name for her husband. It just grew from there."

"So, who does what in King Oil?"

"The Baron still heads up the business, but Duke actually runs the show—although neither one of them will admit it. Dare—the brother I bought the moccasins for—runs all over the world putting out oil-rig fires."

"And what do you do?"

He shot her a wicked grin. "I guess you could say I just run." It was the truth. In eighth grade he'd realized that the only way to make things happen was to be in charge, so he'd planned to run for office. He'd been a congressman for three years. Ironically the election had also cost him his family.

"After beautiful women, I suspect."

His grin faded. "At this very moment, I'm keeping company with one of the two most beautiful women I've ever met."

Kristi gulped, then recovered her aplomb. "Who's the other?" she asked cheekily.

"My grandmother. You're a lot like her." He gazed at Kristi thoughtfully, becoming very much aware of her resemblance to his grandmother. It wasn't a physical resemblance but an inner beauty—an inner conviction—that gave them a similar glow. A glow he hadn't seen in any of the women he'd dated. "She's been after me to get busy and produce a great-grandchild. She's given up on my brothers," he blurted out, then cleared his throat in embarrassment. Now why in the devil did he have to go and say that? Kristi looked as if she were ready to jump overboard and swim for shore, or at least sic her dog on him.

"I hate to think what she'd want to call the poor child," Kristi muttered. Reeling in her line, she picked up the bag of doughnuts. She selected one coated with sugar and cinnamon. "So are you married?" she asked, passing him the bag.

Marriage had been in the back of his mind for the last few months. He was lonely and needed a wife to work beside him, especially now that he was entering the senatorial race. "No," he said softly. "Are you?"

"Nope." Confused by the quick rush of pleasure that had accompanied his words, she turned her attention to the doughnuts.

Gripping the rod under his arm, Dev reached into the bag, then paused, his gaze riveted on Kristi. Eyes closed in pure enjoyment, she daintily nibbled around the outer edge of the doughnut. Dev forgot to breathe as he imagined her nibbling him. Rolling the sweetness in her mouth, she savored it thoroughly, then swallowed. If he'd known how much she enjoyed doughnuts he'd have brought a dozen, no a hundred, he thought wildly. Doughnut consumed, she slowly sucked the sugar from her forefinger. Her finger emerged with a plop, and she glanced up at him and smiled her thanks.

"Hmmm, delicious."

Dev gazed at her, his heart thumping, his blood pounding, his whole body throbbing, then suddenly his fishing rod jerked. The bag went flying as he grabbed for the reel, burning his thumb on the singing line. He reared back, cranking furiously, uncaring that the canoe was tipped dangerously or that Rex was barking in excitement. No way was he going to lose the rod. Or the fish.

Laughing, Kristi quickly braced her hands on the gunnels to steady the rocking canoe. Her laughter died as Rex leaned over, snatched the bag out of the water, and dropped it in Dev's lap. With his knees splayed against the sides of the canoe, Dev was wide open for viewing. Her eyes grew larger as she realized what the bulging denim concealed.

Feeling decidedly uncomfortable, she took refuge in words. "Tip us over, and you're a dead duck."

Dev didn't answer. His thigh muscles tightened and relaxed as he worked the rod back and forth. Forcing her gaze upward, Kristi concentrated on Dev's face. His hair, burnished to copper by the sun, fell in unruly waves over his forehead. Eyes the color of a lily pond in the deep forest gleamed with determination. And he was smiling, a wide smile of sheer enjoyment, a smile that crinkled every laughter line on his face. A smile that played a tune on her heartstrings.

"You want help landing that thing?" she asked breathlessly.

"No way. I'll do this myself."

With a loud splash, the fish leapt into the air. Shaking free of the hook, it landed in Dev's lap. Dev stared down at the fish, a look of stunned amazement on his face.

"Big, huh?"

Kristi choked. "I'll say."

The fish flopped into the bottom of the canoe, covering Dev's jeans with scales and slime. Kristi's eyes followed its progress.

"Must be all of fifty pounds," Dev said proudly.

"T-try twenty."

"Well, anyway, it's pretty good for my first fish."

Kristi laughed. She couldn't help it. Dev looked so pleased with himself. "Yeah, you're a real pro. I think we'll call it a day. It's big enough to feed the three of us."

"You're sure? Now that I've got the hang of it, I could catch another real quick."

"I believe you, but let's give the poor fish a break."

"What kind is it?" he asked, moving his foot out of the way of the slapping tail.

She hesitated a moment. "A great northern pike."

He eyed her thoughtfully. "Isn't that another name for the fish you threw back earlier?"

"I guess so," she muttered, then shaking her head at her softhearted foolishness, she picked up her paddle and turned the canoe for shore.

A warm feeling—one that he associated with sitting on the Duchess's knee when he was a child—swept through Dev and settled in the region of his heart. Kristi Bjornson was a very caring lady. Why else would she worry about spoiling his small triumph?

She glanced up at him shyly, and he cocked his head and slanted her a slow, thankful smile. It was kind of nice to have someone care about him again—and he almost told her so, but he didn't want to embarrass her any further. After savoring the good feelings for a few more moments he reluctantly put them in safekeeping . . . somewhere close to his heart.

"You can take us home, James," he said huskily, then stowed his rod and rescued the bag of doughnuts from under Rex's leg. Removing one, he gingerly fed the soggy mess to the dog, then selected another and bit into it. The taste of sugar on his tongue brought back the memory of Kristi eating dough-nuts, and with it the pleasant ache of arousal.

Leaning back, he trailed his hand in the cold water and gazed at Kristi. Her hair glowed like a golden torch against the sky. Her blue eyes sparkled brightly in her tanned face. Her red lips were parted in a happy smile as she effortlessly paddled the canoe. She had a natural rhythm, a confidence and grace that made each movement a thing of beauty. The thought of her moving above him with the same rhythm and beauty brought a new surge of blood to his loins.

He raised his eyes to hers, making no effort to hide his desire, since his body was bent on showing her just how much he wanted her. Dev caught a glimpse of something in her eyes before she looked down at the paddle.

He laughed softly as her cheeks grew pink. Maybe the lady wasn't the self-confident icemaiden that she was pretending to be. Maybe she was just a little bit interested in him. Maybe after he'd sweet-talked her into letting him put up the marker, he could get rid of the dog and steal a kiss.

Four

Getting rid of Rex was easier said than done, Dev realized as he swallowed the last piece of fish. The dog was sitting with his head on Kristi's knee, gazing at her with soulful eyes, begging for scraps. Not that he could blame Rex. Kristi cooked a mean fish. He'd helped by cleaning it, and the fact that she had tolerated his inexperience without a word of ridicule had left him with another warm glow in the region of his heart.

But he didn't want to examine the feelings she inspired in him. All he wanted was to convince her to let him erect the marker the following day so he could leave. And to do that he'd have to learn more about this intriguing woman—find out what made her tick, her strengths and weaknesses. Not that she had any weakness he could see.

Except for oranges. Perched on the campstool she was carefully cleaning the insides of a third orange peel. He grinned at the memory of how quickly she'd finished the first orange and how eagerly she'd accepted the second. Although more embarrassed about the third, she'd eaten it with as much enjoyment. He suspected Kristi enjoyed many things in life, and he half envied the lucky man who would share her pleasure.

"Tell me about the work you've done, Kristi," he asked, watching with fascination as her darting tongue wiped juice from her lips.

Kristi glanced at him from under lowered lashes as she slowly sucked the sweetness off her fingers. This was as good a time as any to try and convert Dev.

A smug smile tugged the corner of her mouth. She was so beautiful, it was all Dev could do to keep from kissing the smile off her face. Come to think of it, he didn't want her to stop smiling—especially after he'd kissed her. He wanted her to grin like a Cheshire cat.

Her smile faded to a wary expression, and he realized his intentions couldn't have been more blatant than if he'd shouted them to the sky. Lord, he'd have to go slow, or she'd tell him to pack up and leave.

"I really am interested," he prompted.

She took a deep breath, warning her pounding heart to behave or she'd put it on ice. "Right now we're finishing up a three-year research project on the survival rates of Tundra Swans. We've also studied the nesting habits of the whooping crane in Wood Buffalo National Park. And we spent a number of years plotting the migratory patterns of Canada geese and Tundra Swans."

"You've done all that!" Dev asked in disbelief, then gave a whoop of elation. Damn, but his luck was holding. He'd come north to put the marker on his grandfather's grave, despite the fact he should be in Washington looking for someone to head his Wildfowl Task Force. And eureka, he'd just found his expert.

Easy there, he told himself, aware that Kristi was staring at him as though he'd gone completely bonkers. She might not be the right person for the job. He had to get the facts first, before he made his decision.

"Bjornson. Your father is Ken Bjornson?" he asked, suddenly remembering where he'd heard the name before.

"Yes," she said, still confused by his reaction.

"He travels all over the country giving lectures on wildfowl, doesn't he?"

"Yes. There's not much money in field research, you know, and it's one way of making ends meet. Besides, it's an important way to reach people, to make them aware of the problems the birds are facing."

"And you've gone on tour with him?"

"I started traveling with him when I was thirteen, and I still go along whenever I can take time away from my graduate studies. He does all the talking, though. As I said before, I hate speaking in public."

"You've been to college?" Dev asked, zeroing in on the one piece of information that interested him. Degrees held more weight than experience when it came to impressing his colleagues.

"I'm just completing my masters in arctic biology."

"A masters! I'm impressed. Have you written any articles about your work?" he asked, hoping against hope she had. Publishing credits were even more important, especially if she'd published in *The National Geographic*, his colleagues' favorite source of information.

"Hundreds." She smiled impishly. "Not quite that many, but a few dozen."

"You wouldn't happen to have any with you?" He held his breath while he waited for her answer. If he could just read some of them, he'd know whether he could offer her the job.

"As a matter of fact, I do," she said, feeling slightly embarrassed. She didn't normally haul her articles around with her, but she was working on her thesis and needed them for references.

He exhaled slowly. "I'd like to read them."

"Now?" she asked, surprised and flattered by his interest.

"You bet." Rising to his feet, he pulled her up. "Go get them."

She laughed softly. "You were sitting on them."

Bending over, Dev lifted the lid of the wooden crate and removed a cardboard box, then sank back down on his seat with the box on his knee.

"Is this a ploy to get out of washing dishes?" Kristi asked.

Dev didn't answer, and Kristi stared at him in astonishment. His head was already bowed over a magazine article. Obviously he hadn't even heard her.

"The first time I have company all summer, and what does he do but read." she grumbled, scraping the leftovers into Rex's bowl.

After storing the food, she began the dishes, stepping over and around Dev, who ignored her completely. As she worked she studied him, wondering why he was so interested in the reports.

"Terrific," he muttered.

"What is?" she asked, placing the frying pan into the other storage box and closing the lid.

More silence. Making a face at him, Kristi picked up the logbook and sank down on the campstool.

Suddenly she wondered if Dev thought he could find something in those articles to discredit her work. That would be difficult. The only study that was even questionable was the present project with the Tundra Swans. The shy, elusive birds were difficult to spot when they were nesting, but she seemed to have an inborn ability to locate their nests. Maybe because she felt as shy as the Tundra Swans, especially around men.

And her one experience with a man had been a disaster. Fergus had won her trust, then used her, and in the process had left her with a deep-seated skepticism about men.

Especially men like Dev. With his good looks and potent charm, he'd probably left a string of broken hearts all over the lower forty-eight. Yes, Dev was a rake. She'd stake the rest of the oranges on it.

"Fantastic."

This time she didn't bother to respond as Dev laid down one article and picked up another. He was totally oblivious to her.

Which didn't do much for her ego, she acknowledged wryly. Especially since she she had to admit there was something about Dev that appealed to her and that she couldn't ignore. She couldn't put a finger on it, but it was there.

Kristi snorted as she admitted it was probably a good dose of lust. His snug-fitting jeans made his endowments so apparent, she'd found it impossible not to stare while she'd paddled back to shore. And to her discomfort, the looking had brought with it an excitement and a warmth she hadn't felt in a long time.

Yes, the man was dangerous—but it wasn't only Dev she had to worry about, it was her reaction to him.

Dev raised his head and gazed at her, his green eyes glowing with an intensity that made her blood simmer. If that wasn't bad enough, he gave her a slow, sexy smile, and something inside her began to fizz. What did he want? she wondered. And what was she prepared to give him?

"I've got to have you, Kristi," he said, his voice full of entreaty.

Kristi stared at Dev in surprise. "What?" she croaked, afraid he'd suddenly lost his mind or, worse yet, that she'd lost hers.

"You're just the person I've been looking for."

His smile widened, but this time Kristi didn't see the creases, only the beguiling charm. "And just what do you mean by that?" she demanded, rising abruptly to her feet.

Dev rose to stand beside her. "These reports are very impressive, Kristi," he said, waving a copy of *The National Geographic* at her. "With your knowledge of migratory waterfowl and the Mississippi and Central flyways, you'd be perfect for my project."

Kristi stared at him, feeling a bitter taste of disappointment in the base of her throat as she realized Dev was setting her up. King Oil wasn't out to discredit her work, they were going to try and buy her off.

"What project?" she asked, deciding to wait until he asked her to work for King Oil before telling him to go to Siberia and take his job offer with him.

"I'm chairing a commission which will make recommendations on the drainage of the wetlands along the Gulf Coast."

His words were totally unexpected. "Drain the wetlands!" She stepped forward, hands on hips. "Why, that's absolutely criminal! What's going to happen to the birds?"

He smiled at her reaction, hoping he had her hooked. "The birds are only one aspect of the commission. There are farming, fishing, and industrial interests to be considered," he said as he carefully replaced the articles in the box.

"Just where do you stand on the issue?"

"I'm for finding a balance that will protect the environment and wildlife."

"That's difficult to swallow. You're an oilman."

He shook his head. "My father's the oilman."

She dismissed that with a wave of her hand. "Well, it's the same thing. How did you get to be chairman? And what kind of commission is it, anyway?"

"Congressional."

Eyes wide, she rocked back on her heels. "You're a congressman?"

He smiled at the incredulity in her voice. "Yes."

"I don't believe it."

Suddenly her constant disbelief was no longer

funny. "What proof do you need?" Pulling his billfold from the front pocket of his bomber jacket, he found a card and handed it to her. "Is this enough?"

Kristi glanced down at the embossed royal-blue script. If he wasn't a congressman, he'd sure gone to a lot of expense to print cards. Well, congressmen could be bought. Especially one who had such close ties to the oil industry. And obviously the Baron thought she could be bought too. There was no doubt in her mind that the job offer was really a bribe to keep her from opposing King Oil.

"Okay, so you're a congressman," she said, returning the card.

Cocking his head, he gave her a coaxing smile. "So, will you work for me?"

"Nope."

"Why not?" he asked, disappointed she hadn't readily agreed to his plans. Certainly there might be a few people who were better qualified for the job, but he'd have to look long and hard to find them. And why bother? He couldn't go wrong hiring Kristi. As long as he kept their relationship on a professional basis, he reminded himself.

Kristi watched as Dev's smile faded into sober determination. There was definitely more to this man—this congressman—than his good looks.

"You politicians are all the same," she said, ignoring for now her suspicion that Dev was really working for his father. "You're full of high ideals and talk, but short on works and money. When it comes down to the crunch, money is scarcer than trees on the tundra."

"Now just a minute—"

"No, you hear me out. I've seen project after project canceled because they were dependent on government funding, and someone with a vested interest put the screws on someone else. How much do you want to bet they'll even pull the plug on *your* project?" She raised her hand as he attempted to speak again. "No way do I want my blood, sweat, and tears to become a political football."

"But I don't understand," he said, impatiently shoving his wallet into his pocket. "You care what happens to the birds, don't you?"

"Of course."

"Well, I'm giving you a chance to do something about their plight. I want you to head up the Waterfowl Task-Force which will be reporting directly to the commission."

Kristi was sorely tempted. This was what she'd worked for all her life—the opportunity to have a meaningful impact on the preservation of waterfowl. But as much as she wanted to take the job, she couldn't. However it was packaged, she'd be accepting a bribe.

Besides, it would entail making speeches, and after the botch she'd made at the environmental hearing, she'd vowed she'd never give another speech, especially when someone was depending on her to come through with the goods.

She raised her chin a notch. "I can't take the job," she said with quiet finality in her voice.

"Why not?" he persisted. Kristi was the most bullheaded woman he'd run into in a long time—except for the Duchess when it came to the topic of great-grandchildren. Come to think of it, he was seeing more and more of his grandmother in Kristi with each passing minute. And his grandmother was one grand lady.

Kristi watched as Dev's eyes began to take on an expression that made her feel special—as if she were the only woman in the world.

"I . . . I have other obligations."

"What is so important that you'd give up an opportunity to do something for your birds?"

Damn. He knew all the right buttons to push, which didn't make it any easier to keep refusing. "It's none of your business," she said abruptly.

"A man?"

"No." As soon as the word was out of her mouth, Kristi regretted it. She could use a fictional lover right now to keep this sexy man at arm's length. At double arm's length—hers as well as Dev's.

"Whew." He wiped the back of his hand across his brow in an exaggerated gesture of relief. "Thank goodness I don't have to worry about that," he said, his mouth curving into an engaging smile. "Look, Kristi. I really do want you to work for me."

Kristi shook her head at his antics. How could she remain angry with Dev when he was such a charmer? "Sorry. No deal."

"Is there any way I can convince you?"

"Nope."

Suddenly bone weary, Dev rubbed his hand over his face. Somehow he had to persuade her to change her mind, but right now he was too tired to plan tactics. He'd try again first thing in the morning.

As his hand dropped away from his face Kristi noticed the purple shadows beneath his eyes. "When did you sleep last?"

"I don't remember. It's hard to keep track of time up here in the land of the midnight sun."

Smiling at the *cheechako*'s words, Kristi glanced around, drinking in the beauty that never failed to move her. Twilight surrounded them, descending from the sky in a shimmering haze to rest in a pool of molten gold on the nearby lake.

Everything seemed more golden this night, and Kristi wondered why. Her eyes sought the man standing silently beside her while her mind refused to accept that she was looking at the reason. Out on the lake a loon called to his mate, his plaintive voice touching the depths of her loneliness. Beside her, Dev shivered.

"You're cold," Kristi said softly.

He rubbed his hands up and down the sleeves of

his leather jacket. "I haven't really warmed up since I went wading after my plane."

"And I didn't help matters by taking you fishing," she said, resisting the sudden unexplainable urge to gather him in her arms and warm him up. She wrapped her arms around her waist instead. "I think you should hit the sack."

Dev stared at Kristi, remembering his earlier vow to steal a kiss from her. He hadn't had any luck convincing her to come work for him, however he wasn't about to give up on the kiss.

"Would you do something for me before I go to bed?" he asked, gazing at her soulfully.

Dropping her arms to her sides, Kristi moved closer, drawn by the entreaty in his face. "What?"

"Don't look so suspicious. It's a harmless request."

The boyish smile flashed again, and she couldn't help but smile back as she asked, "What?"

"Will you kiss me goodnight?"

"You call that harmless?"

"Perfectly. I won't lay a hand on you. Rex will make sure of that."

Linking his hands together behind his back, he bowed his head. His eyes were closed and his lips curved in a half smile, almost as if he were expecting a reward for being good, Kristi thought. One little kiss wouldn't hurt, would it?

"Oh, what the heck." Rising on her toes, Kristi brushed her lips against his. With a coaxing movement, his lips encouraged hers to stay and explore. They felt so warm, so good, she forgot her intention to keep the kiss brief. She nibbled at their fullness, then paused as he sighed softly. Again she felt the urge to touch him and knew she missed touching as much as talking. Giving in to the urge, she twined her hands around his head and pulled it down.

The kiss warmed every nerve ending in her body. Her heart thumped wildly, like a runaway propeller, and the world spun in circles. She closed her eyes, reveling in the stimulating sensations, wanting more. When she increased her demand, his lips responded. Under her foolhardy wanting was something else, she realized—a yearning that had been aching to make itself known all evening. The yearning was dangerous, more so than the wanting. It could lead to deep, deep trouble.

He was in deep, deep trouble, Dev thought. One taste of Kristi's orange-flavored lips, and he wanted to crush her in his arms and never let her go. He moaned, gripping his hands tighter behind his back, knowing that if he even so much as relaxed one finger, he'd never be able to keep his promise not to touch her.

Kristi heard the moan and wondered if it had come from her. She pressed closer, wanting to get under his skin. Suddenly the full impact of what she was doing stung her like buckshot. Dev wasn't touching her, but she was doing more than enough touching for both of them.

Releasing him, she stepped back and glared at him, expecting to see him gloating. He looked absolutely stunned. Slowly, he raised his hand and brushed his bent thumb across his lips.

Kristi rubbed hers furiously and blurted out the first words that came to mind. "You don't call that dangerous? You should declare your lips a lethal weapon."

"And the touch of your lips is enough to make a man go up in smoke," Dev said hoarsely. Slowly, his senses still reeling, he reached out and touched Kristi's lips with a finger that trembled.

She gasped and stepped backward, and it took every tattered ounce of Dev's willpower to keep from sweeping her into his arms and kissing her again and again until neither one of them had any willpower left. But she was alone, he reminded himself, and vulnerable, and no way did he want to frighten her.

Giving Kristi a contrite smile, he solemnly laid his hand over his heart, and felt the box in his breast pocket. The pendant would definitely suit Kristi, he thought in bemusement. It was almost as if it had been carved especially for her. Was that why he'd made a special trip back into the shop to buy it? Was the midnight sun casting a spell? he wondered as he bunched the leather into the palm of his hand and gripped the pendant firmly.

Kristi eyed his hand nervously, but held her ground. "I bet the Washington gossip columns run a story every morning about the dashing Devlin King and the beautiful woman he was dating the night before."

Dev hung his head, wishing there were some way of evading the truth. But he wasn't going to start lying now, he decided, looking her straight in the eye. "Not every morning."

"Well, there aren't reporters out here, and I'm not going to line up for another kiss."

He laughed softly. "You don't have to stand in line, Kristi, I'd be happy to kiss you anytime you want, anyplace you want."

"I bet you say that to all your women."

"I've never said those words before," he said, and realized immediately that it was true. Not one of the Washington socialites had left him as breathless as Kristi had.

"Soft words won't get you anywhere with this backwoods gal."

"You want more action? I'll be happy to oblige." He took a step forward, then halted midstride when Rex growled. "Look, Kristi. You're perfectly safe with me," he said, taking a firmer grip on the pendant.

Kristi studied him, uncertain if she should believe him. Maybe he wouldn't deliberately hurt her, but if she wasn't careful, she could easily get caught in his seductive web.

"Oh, go to bed, Tenderfoot."

His eyes grew heavy lidded as they drifted slowly to her lips and lingered for long moments. She held her breath, wondering what she would do if he tried to kiss her again.

"Yes, ma'am," he said softly, then turned away, leaving Kristi totally confused.

Kristi lay in her sleeping bag, staring wide-eyed at the tent roof, seeking answers to the turmoil in her mind. Why was she feeling this way? Acting this way? Why had she agreed to kiss Dev, then attacked him as though she were starving for love?

And why did Dev have to be so nice? Womanizers were supposed to have horns or snake skins, not misty green eyes and a kiss that turned her into a quivering mass of yearning. No wonder the women in Washington were smitten. She could just see them now, hanging on to his arm and gazing up at him as if he were a king.

But he was a King. Which made it totally impossible to take the job. The offer had been tempting, but it was too suspicious coming right on the heels of the oil spill, her father's accident, and her letter. She saw the Baron's fine hand in it, backed by the iron fist of the Duke. Maybe Dev was an innocent pawn, but she didn't want to be around when King Oil made the sweep of the chessboard.

One injured Bjornson was enough.

Tears stung her eyes as she remembered how close she'd come to losing her father. Oh how she missed him. She'd never thought about loneliness before. She'd always loved the silence of the North.

Suddenly the silence was shattered by a noise. Kristi elbowed upright, listening. At the foot of the bed, Rex raised his head and whined. It came again, a long, drawn-out sound that ended with a snort. Dev snored!

Flopping back on her pillow, Kristi waited for the

next one. It came, louder and longer. The following three were just as bad. How in the devil was she ever going to sleep with all that racket? No wonder he wasn't married!

Sitting bolt upright, she yelled, "Roll over." Rex barked his agreement.

There was silence for thirty seconds, then the snoring began again. Throwing aside the covers, Kristi pulled her Eskimo parka shell over her long johns, shoved her feet into moccasins, and crawled outside.

Crossing the short distance between the tents, she entered Dev's and crouched down beside him. The twilight filtered through the blue nylon, casting a gloom. Dev lay on his back, his head lolled, his mouth open. A deep, sonorous sound came from his throat.

Kristi sank onto her heels as he suddenly pushed back the down-filled sleeping bag. He was naked. At least to the waist. She forced her eyes to remain on his chest. It was tanned, muscular, and just the right amount of hair tapered down—no, she wouldn't look.

She stared at his face instead. Such a handsome face. Such innocent eyes. Such a soft, sexy mouth.

Holy hat! What was she doing, gazing at Dev as though she were a love-struck groupie with a crush on a rock star. She was twenty-six for heaven's sake.

Enough of this, she decided. She reached out a hand to shake him, then stopped. It really would be a shame to wake him. He looked so tired, and he'd probably start snoring again before she got out of the tent. Oh, what the heck, she'd let him sleep.

She turned to leave, then swung back as if drawn by the magnetic north pole. He shivered, and she felt an overwhelming urge to crawl into the sleeping bag and share her body heat with him—she had more than enough of it to go around. She remained motionless for a long moment, fighting the trembling feeling that filled her body.

Damn her wayward senses! He'd have to go.

It no longer mattered whether he was working for his father or if he *really* was there to put a marker on his grandfather's grave. Nor did it matter whether she could convert him into an environmentalist or if he had already taken up the cause. What did matter was the way her traitorous body was reacting to him. She'd send him packing in the morning.

He shivered but made no move to pull up the covers. Carefully she drew the sleeping bag over him. He stopped midsnore, wiggled his nose, then turned over onto his side. Kristi waited, barely breathing, until he'd settled down, then silently crept outside.

Halfway to her tent she realized the ramifications of her decision. She might have enough willpower to tell Dev to leave, but not if he took the oranges with him. Crossing to the pingo, she opened the door and retrieved the paper bag. Inside her tent once more she wriggled into the sleeping bag, gave Rex an absent pat, then began eating.

The oranges satisfied one need but another began to grow as she thought about sending Dev on his way. Surely she wasn't going to miss the *cheechako*?

She'd only known him a few hours.

Five

Kristi glanced up from the camp stove as Dev staggered out of his tent. In stocking feet, with half-closed eyes and tousled hair, he looked as harmless as a little boy. A boy he's not, Kristi reminded herself briskly. He's a sexy man, a charming man, a dangerous man.

"You'll have to leave today," she said abruptly.

Dev's mouth closed around a yawn, then opened in surprise. "What?"

"You'll have to go back to Fairbanks to wait."

Sleepily, he rubbed his jaw. "Can we discuss this after I've put on my boots and had a cup of coffee?"

"We can discuss it, but I won't change my mind."

Shaking his head as if still trying to clear the cobwebs, he ambled toward the lake. Rex trotted behind, his tail waving like a plume.

Kristi stared at Dev's back, wondering why she was already feeling lonely. Sighing, she turned her attention to the black-bottom pot and absently stirred the oatmeal.

Dev's muffled curse and Rex's yelp sent Kristi flying to the shore. Dev sat on the bank, his bloody right foot propped on his left thigh.

"What happened?" she asked, as she dropped to

her knees beside him and began removing his sock.

"I stepped on something. A fish scaler, I think," he muttered, vaguely aware that Rex had moved closer and was gazing at him anxiously.

Kristi spared him a glance that more than matched her dog's. "Of all the stupid stunts!"

"No need to tell me. And no need to remind me that it was I who cleaned the fish and left the knife lying on the ground."

Sock off, she examined the wound. "This needs stitches."

He squinted at it. "It's fine. If you'll just give me something to stop the bleeding, I'll manage."

"Hold your foot up," she ordered. "I'll be right back." Rising to her feet, she covered the distance to her plane in three strides, jumped onto the float, and removed the first-aid kit from the baggage compartment. At his side once more, she opened the kit and unwrapped a pad of gauze. Carefully she clamped the pad over the wound and applied pressure.

"You really are a tenderfoot. Do you feel faint?"

"No, but even if I did, I don't have far to fall," he said, an ironic smile hovering on his lips.

Forcing her gaze away from his lips and her mind from the memory of how they'd made her tremble, she added another pad to the wound.

"I'd better fly you out to the hospital before you bleed to death."

She wasn't going to get rid of him that easily, Dev thought, peering into the kit. "I see you're carrying sutures. Have you ever sewed up anyone?"

"Only Rex, but before you get any ideas, I should warn you that I don't have any novocaine."

Dev absently patted the dog's head, which was now resting on his thigh. "If Rex can stand it, so can I."

Kristi wondered if *she* could, but she knew she had no choice. The rate his blood was flowing, he wouldn't have enough left to donate by the time they arrived in Fairbanks.

With shaking fingers, she opened the sterile forceps and suture. Taking a deep breath, she pulled off the pad and stared down at the wound. She wouldn't think about Dev. Wouldn't think about how much she was hurting him. The needle pierced his already scarred flesh. He flinched but kept his foot motionless. Sudden tears blurred her vision. Blinking them away, she made the tie, then took another stitch.

Dev buried his hand in Rex's hair and tried to ignore the bite of the needle by watching Kristi instead. She was obviously upset because she was hurting him, yet she was bravely doing what she could to help. Lips pressed tightly together, she concentrated on her task. Her long, slender fingers were firm but gentle, quick but sure. Fingers meant to touch a man in love, not in pain.

No, not *a* man. Him.

Damn. Where had that thought come from? Hadn't he vowed that he wouldn't get involved with a crusader again? But the very qualities that made Kristi a crusader were the qualities he wanted in the person to head his task force.

Dev gazed at Kristi in bemusement as he waged a silent battle. There was something about Kristi that touched him deeply, and there was something deep inside him that reached out to touch her. Could he risk becoming involved with her, even on a professional basis?

He nodded slightly as he came to a decision. It was no longer important to put up the marker and leave. It was much more important to persuade Kristi to come work with him. And that would take time. It might take every minute of the week he'd originally allotted himself—if Kristi would allow him to stay. For some reason—probably because of the kiss—she'd decided he'd have to leave. After this fiasco she'd send him packing for sure.

With a deep sigh of relief, Kristi snipped the last suture, sank back on her heels, and hid her trembling hands between her thighs. Quickly Dev leaned forward and put an arm around her shoulders. "There, that wasn't so bad, was it?"

His gentle voice and solid arm cut through Kristi's haze of panic. "Easy for you to say. All you had to do was sit there," she muttered, resting her head against his shoulder.

His rich laughter broke the stillness of the morning. "Hey. Hey. Don't be so upset." He gave her a reassuring hug, liking the way her head nestled against his shoulder. "You did a terrific job. You can patch me up anytime you want to."

For a few weak moments Kristi rested in the comfort of his arms, then forced herself to move away to finish the job. She stared down at the mass of scars which covered his foot and shuddered. "Thank goodness I didn't have to stitch that mess! What happened?" she asked, dabbing at the dried blood with an alcohol-soaked pad.

He sucked in a sharp breath as the alcohol ran into the wound, then let it out slowly. "I made the mistake of getting mixed up in a dogfight when I was a kid."

She picked up the roll of gauze and began bandaging the wound. "Why would you do such a foolish thing?"

"Buttons was my grandmother's dog. I didn't even like her. She was a yappy thing and constantly nipped at my heels." He shrugged. "But it was the first winter after the King had crashed, and when a pack of dogs attacked her, I couldn't just stand aside and do nothing." He gave a short laugh. "Afterwards, Buttons still tried to bite me every chance she could get."

A fluttery warmth filled Kristi's chest. Somehow it didn't surprise her that Dev, the boy, put himself at risk to rescue Buttons. She wouldn't put it past Dev, the man, to attempt the same feat, only on a larger scale, if he thought something or someone was in danger. "I don't imagine you've learned your lesson, have you?"

"I usually wear boots. And I have a healthy fear of dogs." He glanced down in amazement at his hand, which was buried in Rex's hair. The dog stared up at him with soft brown eyes, then raised his muzzle and swiped a long tongue across his cheek. Dev gave a startled laugh but didn't retreat from Rex's flicking tongue, receiving two more licks before the dog dropped his head back on his knee.

The fluttery warmth in Kristi's chest flowed down into the pit of her stomach as she watched the interplay between the man and dog. "I can see that," she said.

"Well, Rex is different. I think he likes me."

No wonder, Kristi thought, lowering her gaze to her hands. After strapping a piece of tape around the gauze, she rose to her feet. "I hate to tell you this, but you'll have to wear your moccasins again today. Where are they?"

He groaned. "I had hoped I'd never have to wear them again so I buried them deep in the bag of souvenirs."

She returned in due course with a pair of socks and the moccasins dangling from the tips of two fingers.

Dev gave Rex a final pat, then caught Kristi's free hand and gazed up at her in concern. "Kristi, I've been sitting here wondering what you would've done if you'd cut your foot and there was no one around to help you."

Surprised, Kristi could only stand and stare down at him. "I guess I'd have to sew it myself."

"But you might be injured so badly that you wouldn't be able to fly your plane. What would you do then?"

"I'd wait around camp until my foot healed, or

someone flew in to check on me. People do drop by, you know." She gave a little tug of her hand, trying to free it.

He wouldn't let go. "What if you chopped your foot with the ax? You'd bleed to death before you could get to the first-aid kit."

"For heaven sake, Dev, stop worrying about me. Even my father doesn't make this much fuss about leaving me alone."

She pulled harder this time, making Dev aware that he was holding her. Reluctantly he released her, and she quickly shoved the moccasins and socks into his outstretched hand.

"Well, I don't like the idea of you flying around the North all by yourself, and if you were my daughter or wife, you sure as hell wouldn't be here," he said, frustrated because he couldn't keep her safe.

"Thank goodness I'm neither," she said as the warm feeling invaded the pit of her stomach again. It was kind of nice to have someone worrying about her for a change . . . even if that someone was a King. She shook her head in disgust, wondering why she was feeling so weak all of a sudden. It must be hunger, she told herself, then remembered the breakfast she'd left simmering on the camp stove. "I'll go rescue the oatmeal. Can you make it back to the kitchen?"

With a sigh of resignation, Dev began easing a clean sock over his bandaged foot. "I'm sure I can hobble that far, but I don't think I should fly for a few days. I could manage once I was in the air, but the takeoff and landing would put too much pressure on the wound. It would be a shame to pop these stitches after you worked so hard to put them in." As he reached for the other sock, he noticed a wary expression on her face. "Do you really thing I'd go to this much trouble to hang around camp?"

"The thought crossed my mind."

"There are easier ways to convince you to let me

stay," he said, then realizing it probably wasn't the best time to tease Kristi, he gave her a coaxing grin. "You are going to let me stay, aren't you?"

Kristi hastily averted her eyes from the smile that was doing shameless things to her body, reminding her why she'd told him to leave. If she knew what was good for her, she'd fly the charming congressman out to Fairbanks before she succumbed completely to his sweet talk and his smile. But she didn't have the time to spare. Fall and the fog were only a few days away, and she had to finish the count before then.

"I don't want to leave," he prompted, his grin fading, his eyes compelling her to agree.

Reluctantly Kristi gave in to the pull of his gaze. As she stared into his moss-green eyes, she made the startling discovery that her answer meant a great deal to Devlin King. And she also made the equally startling discovery that she didn't have the heart to insist that he leave.

"Okay, you can stay," she said huskily. Picking up the first-aid kit, she beat a hasty retreat before she did something foolish—like kiss him.

Rex followed, then stopped to wait for Dev. Bent over the stove once more, Kristi eyed her traitorous dog. Even Rex was turning mushy on her.

"Why did you decide I had to leave today?" Dev asked as he settled onto one wooden crate and propped his foot up on the other. Rex plunked down between his legs and laid his head against his left knee.

"I had second thoughts." Kristi turned from the camp stove, took one look at the way Dev's jeans hugged his muscular thighs, and had third thoughts.

Keeping her eyes averted, she handed him a mug of coffee and a bowl of oatmeal, then accidentally-on-purpose kicked over her campstool. Righting it, she sat down as far from Dev as possible and called

Rex to her side. When the dog had settled on the ground beside the stool, she finally glanced at the man who so disturbed her senses. He was watching her with a knowing look that said, *You don't fool me one little bit.*

Kristi lowered her gaze to her oatmeal, totally aware of Dev as he spooned two sugars into his coffee, drank it thirstily, and began eating his oatmeal.

"Because of the kiss?" he asked quietly.

"Among other things," she said, her breath catching in her throat. Just his words were enough to rekindle the warmth and excitement of the kiss.

"It was a terrific kiss, wasn't it?"

Terrific! It was stupendous . . . and downright scary, she thought.

"It . . ." She cleared her throat. "It was okay."

"Only okay?" He pulled a sad face. "That's not good enough. What say I try for excellent?"

She edged the stool back farther. "No way."

He sighed, disappointed in her reaction to his gentle teasing. "You don't trust me, do you, Kristi?"

"No, I don't." Much less herself, she admitted silently.

"Because of the kiss?"

"Because you're a King," she said, dredging up the real reason from its hiding place in the back of her mind. Damn, it was getting more and more difficult to keep remembering King Oil's involvement in the oil spill and her father's accident.

"Because I'm a King?" he asked, puzzled by her response.

"Yes."

He waited for her to elaborate, and when she didn't he frowned down at his empty bowl. Why didn't she trust him? The question begged to be asked, but now was not the time. She was barely tolerating his presence. No telling what she'd do if he pressed for an answer.

Thoughtfully he placed the bowl on the table and refilled his mug. He cupped it in his still cold hands, raised it for a fortifying drink, then looked at her over the rim. "Come work with me, Kristi, and learn what *this* King is all about. You might even like what you learn."

She stared at him, knowing that despite her previous self-admonishment she was already well on the way to liking this particular King. Which didn't please her one little bit. "I told you last night that I didn't want to work for you," she said abruptly.

"You said you had obligations. What are they?"

For a moment she was tempted to call his bluff and tell him just how she planned to stop King Oil, but decided against it. Why should she tip her hand to the enemy? If he was going to play dumb, she'd play along. And she did have another more immediate, more important obligation.

"I have to finish this project. For my dad's sake. He's depending on me," she said quietly. "No report—no money. And he needs the money to buy a lodge. He plans to turn it into a refuge and cater to guests who are interested in wildlife and conservation." She drained the last of her coffee. "Because of Dad's injury, he can't do fieldwork any longer, so the lodge is extremely important to him. I only hope I can finish the project on time. He's done so much for me. It's the least I can do for him."

Dev gazed at Kristi with growing admiration. Dedication to a cause, commitment in the face of danger, and loyalty to a person were almost as rare as some of the birds Kristi was trying to protect. Kristi possessed these qualities, believed in them, lived by them, and if he had his way, she'd be on the next plane back to Washington. "I can't fault you for standing by your father, Kristi. That's exactly the kind of loyalty I'd want from an employee . . . from a wife."

Kristi shot him a startled glance, then jumped to

her feet. "I can't sit around gabbing about the qualities you require in a wife. I have work to do," she said, as she plopped the dishes into the plastic pan and poured hot water from the kettle over them.

Dev rubbed the back of his neck wearily. *Way to go, King. Way to frighten off the lady.* Where was his so-called charm when he needed it?

Slowly he shoved himself erect, keeping his injured foot propped on the box. "I'll give you a hand with the dishes," he said, leaning over to pick up the dish towel.

Kristi paused, pot in hand, as she watched the way his jeans clung to the trim lines of his pelvis and thighs. Quickly she raked her fingers around the inside of the pot. Nothing like slimy oatmeal to bring a person down to earth, she acknowledged as she emptied the contents into the slop pail. She plunked the pot into the water, wondering why Dev had suddenly gone silent on her.

It was obvious Kristi wasn't going to work for him until he'd won her trust, Dev thought. But how in the devil was he going to accomplish that Herculean feat? With every passing moment he was more determined to have her head his task force. But the moments were passing too quickly, and in this land where day and night blended, it would be easy to lose track of time. He couldn't let her leave him there alone for the entire day.

"I'd also like to help you with the count, Kristi," he said, accepting a spoon she'd fished out of the soapy water. "I'm the first to admit I have a lot to learn about birds, at least on their nesting grounds."

Kristi eyed him with a certain amount of trepidation. She wasn't sure she wanted to be confined in a small plane for hours on end with this sexy man with his heart-stopping body and winning smile. However, if educating him meant the birds on the Gulf Coast would have a better chance of surviving, it would be worth the risk.

"I'd really like to go along, Kristi," Dev said softly.

"Okay, you can come," she said, hoping she wasn't doing something she'd regret.

Nothing could happen in a plane, could it?

During the next five hours Kristi kept one eye on the terrain and the other on Dev, who had insisted on flying the plane once they were airborne. She had expected him to be bored by the tedium of slowly flying back and forth across the endless "wasteland," as he'd called it. Instead, he sat relaxed at the controls, looking as though he had all the time in the world and not another thing to occupy his mind than to keep the plane on course.

She also had to admit that he was a good pilot. At the first nest, she'd put him through a series of turns designed to confuse all but an experienced navigator, and he'd brought the plane around to the same place on the grid. His raised eyebrow told her in no uncertain terms that he was on to her game, but he didn't say a word. Nor did he look smug as he had every right to be. Giving him a contrite smile, she settled down to work. Each time she located a nest she showed it to him, identifying the bird—snowy owl, a Canada goose, a sandhill crane.

When he retrieved his camera from the backseat and began snapping pictures, she was pleased. Dev was definitely hooked.

But so was she, a tiny voice warned her. She had gone past the stage of liking this King a little—she liked him a lot.

If she knew what was good for her, she'd keep him at a distance. However, it was hard to keep him at a distance when they were almost sitting in each other's lap. His broad shoulders stretched his brown sweater to perfection, making her very aware of his latent power. She'd felt it earlier when she'd rested in his arms, but then it had been reassuring. Now it made her realize all too clearly that he was very much a man.

And a very brave man, she thought, remembering the extent of his wound. His foot must be hurting like the devil, but he wasn't saying a word. Just as he hadn't uttered a word of complaint while she'd sewed it up. She had a strong hunch that Dev's brand of courage was much more than feather-deep.

Dev moved his right leg carefully, trying to find a place to prop his foot. It hurt like hell. But what was a little pain if it meant he could have Kristi by his side? And he wouldn't have missed the kiss that had started this mess for all the oil in Alaska. Under Kristi's cool no-nonsense facade lay a very passionate woman, a woman who'd make exploring the lands of love an exciting adventure.

Dammit. He was doing it again. Thinking about making love to this beautiful woman, when he should be concentrating on getting her to work for him. But he couldn't help being totally aware of her when every time she moved her arm it brushed his, or she shifted her leg it nudged his.

Why in the devil was he trying to ignore Kristi when it would be much more fun to explore her? he wondered.

He stole a sidelong glance at her lips, wanting to begin the exploration now. They were so soft, so moist, so enticing, he could spend the rest of the day just charting them. Then he'd move on to her big blue eyes. No, not her eyes. He might get lost in their depths.

He let his gaze drift lower to admire the way her blue chambray shirt molted the fullness of her breasts. It was obvious she wore no bra.

When the throbbing in his loins became more pronounced than the throbbing in his foot, Dev reluctantly forced his gaze back to the instruments. The diversionary tactic didn't work. The throbbing changed to an ache that radiated upward to the region of his heart.

She tapped his arm, and Dev jumped, then tried to pull himself together as she gave him a funny look and pointed to the large lake below where hundreds of swans had congregated in the middle as though attending a convention.

He took a deep, steadying breath. "What's happening?" he asked, tipping the wing of the plane for a better look.

"They're juveniles hanging out for the summer. We'll join them for lunch." Placing her hands on the wheel in front of her, she became the professional pilot. "I'll take over."

"Yes, ma'am," he said, winking broadly as he raised his hands off the dual controls.

She wrinkled her nose at him, then pulled on the flaps and began her descent. The surface of the lake was mirror-smooth, he noticed, making it extremely difficult to judge their height above the water. But she brought the plane down in another perfect landing on the small bay at one end of the lake, barely disturbing the swans.

Kristi cut the engine, letting the momentum of the plane take them into the shallow water.

"We'll eat on land. Would you mind tying up while I take care of some urgent business?"

Before Dev could answer, she'd climbed out on the floats and was wading toward the pebbly beach, the water knee-deep on her hipwaders. He listened to the gyro unwind for the few moments it took Kristi to disappear from sight, then reached into the back of the plane and retrieved his jacket and the waders she'd brought along for him. By the time she returned from her trip over the hill, he'd moored the plane to a rock and had hauled a blanket and the lunch bag ashore.

"Are you all right?" he asked in concern as she

dipped her hands into the water, then dried them by sticking them in her armpits.

She glanced at him through thick lashes. "Yeah."

"Are you sure?"

She sighed. "It's the oranges. The ones you won't be taking home with you." Her cheeks turned a delicate pink under her tan.

"You ate them all?"

"Last night."

"Aha."

"Not another word."

Throwing back his head, Dev laughed in delight. Kristi was such an enchanting mixture. So self-controlled, except when it came to something she enjoyed, then she lost her inhibitions. Making love with her would be an exhilarating experience.

Kristi watched the laughter leave his eyes, replaced by a warm and wanting expression he made no attempt to hide. Turning abruptly, she pointed to a knoll overlooking the larger lake. "Let's eat up there. It should be dry, and it'll give us a better view of the swans. Can you walk that far in those boots?"

"Yes'm," he said, smiling at the way she tried to keep the upper hand by taking charge. He was content to let her take charge—for now.

The knoll was indeed dry and, after removing their hipwaders, they stretched out on the blanket. Kristi took one look at Dev's white face and tight lips, then scrambled around on her hands and knees making a pile of their waders.

"Prop your foot up on that," she ordered.

"Yes'm." This time his smile was one of gratitude as he did what he was told. His foot was throbbing, but gradually the pain abated into a dull ache as they ate lunch. When he spotted a patch of wild blueberries in the nearby grass, she refused to let him move, quickly gathering a cupful. Dev thought they were delicious. But not as delicious as the sight of Kristi's round bottom as she bent over to pick them.

The other throb began again, and Dev deliberately tried to ignore it. "So, are you going to come work with me when your project is finished?"

"You don't give up, do you?"

"When I see what I want, I go after it. And I want you, Kristi." His eyes caressed her. "For the commission. As I said last night, you'd be perfect for the job."

For a moment Kristi let herself bask in his gaze, then she pulled herself back to reality and gave him a wry grin. "No, I wouldn't. I like working alone. I'm not a committee person, and even if I were, I couldn't put up with all the politics that would go with the job." She popped another blueberry into her mouth. "Besides I'd hate to live in a city. I've been in enough of them to know that the concrete, the pollution, the noise, and the people would get to me. Give me the empty tundra anytime."

Dev grinned in amusement at the choice of her words. "Washington is full of trees and parks, you know. And the Chesapeake's in D.C.'s backyard. I occasionally go out there when I want to get away."

She waved her hand toward the swans on the lake. "Maybe you'll see these fine fellows. They winter on the Chesapeake."

"How about that!" He gave her a beguiling smile. "Wouldn't you like to see them in their wintering grounds?"

She smiled back. "Nice try, Dev." She would like to follow the birds south sometime, but she wouldn't stay for long. She loved Alaska and intended on living there the rest of her life, protecting the fragile land from King Oil and the other oil companies who would stop at nothing to make a few more dollars.

Suddenly she remembered her suspicion about the real reason she had been offered the job and wondered where it had been buried these past few hours. Beneath the blanket of Dev's charm, she suspected. "So, tell me, congressman. Why were you appointed to chair the commission?"

"Because I represent one of the regions involved. And I have a reputation for this kind of thing."

"What kind of thing?"

He shrugged. "Never mind. Sorry I mentioned it."

Reaching out, she caught his hand and gave it a squeeze. "Tell me."

Dev gazed down at their hands as he considered his answer. Normally he didn't hold with blowing his own horn, however he did want Kristi to learn more about him and there was no one else around to tell her. "I guess you can say that I've been involved in causes most of my life."

"The crusading congressman with his eyes on the White House?"

"Good Lord, no. I don't need that kind of power. However, I am going to run for the senate next term. Senator Sheldon is retiring, and he and his people want me to take his place."

"Senator! I'm impressed!"

"Well, it isn't in the bag by any means. It's going to take a lot of hard work, but I'm looking forward to the challenge."

"You like the high-flying life, don't you? Parties every night. Dinner with the President."

She stopped as she saw the flicker of amusement in his eyes. "Dev! You are having dinner with the President?"

"A week from Friday."

"No wonder you have to return to Washington." She shook her head. "Well, you can have it. I'd never fit in with the Washington party scene. Being the Iceworm Carnival Queen of Cordova one year was more than enough for me."

"I bet you were the fairest queen they've ever had," Dev said, giving her a look that made her feel beautiful, desirable, and very much a woman.

Flustered, Kristi ducked her head, saw their clasped hands, and abruptly pulled hers away. She was no better than all the Washington women who were dying to sink their talons into this eligible and very handsome bachelor.

Deliberately moving to the edge of the blanket, she stretched out on her side and pillowed her head on her arm. "I think I'll catch a few winks. Someone snored all night and kept me awake."

"I don't snore," he said, wondering what had brought on her quick change of mood.

"Tell that to the birds."

She was asleep almost instantly, giving him the opportunity to watch her. Lord, she was beautiful. Much more beautiful than the women he dated for all their cosmetics and designer gowns. And she'd still be beautiful when she was as old as the Duchess.

Not only was Kristi as beautiful as her grandmother, she had the same strength and courage and sense of humor. Qualities he admired. Qualities that would stand her in good stead in Washington. For despite her assertion that she wasn't right for the job, he knew she would take Washington by storm.

But how was he going to get her to go to Washington?

Searching for answers but lulled by the warmth of the sun, he couldn't think of any . . . couldn't, for the life of him, do anything else but dream. The silence of the land seeped into him, marred only by the plop-plop of water dripping into a nearby pool and the occasional call from a swan on the lake.

Gradually he became aware of the flapping of wings and splashing of webbed feet as the swans chased one another, then retreated. Directly below, two birds swam together looking very much as if they were necking. A third swan approached. The larger of the pair advanced toward it, his body raised, his wings half open. With a powerful bow, he warded off the intruder then glided gracefully back to his mate. Reaching her, he arched his neck and spread his wings, and she accepted him with open wings.

Dev watched another pair of swans repeat the performance, then another, while deep inside a longing flickered, a longing he knew he should smother immediately. Instead it began burning brighter, stronger, purer.

When Kristi stirred, he smiled down at her, his eyes mirroring his turmoil. Slowly she sat up, rubbing a hand across her face to cover a yawn. Without a word he drew her into his arms. She stiffened, then relaxed sleepily against his chest. He held her loosely, afraid he'd frighten her into flight if he made the wrong move. It felt so good to hold her, and he wanted this moment to last forever—even though he knew it wouldn't.

"What's going on out there," he finally whispered. "Are they necking?"

She wiggled her head into the hollow of his shoulder and looked out on the lake. "They're courting," she said, her voice husky with sleep. "Practicing up for the real thing."

"Look. He's defended her and now he's coming back to her all pleased as punch."

"Ummhmm. It's a triumph ceremony—their way of establishing a bond."

Mimicking the actions of the swans, he moved his neck slowly against Kristi's. "You mean he protects her, proves himself to her, and she accepts him?"

"It's all part of the ritual, all part of nature."

"If only it could be as simple for humans," Dev said thoughtfully. If only he could find some way to protect Kristi, maybe he could win her trust. Then maybe she'd come work with him, and maybe . . .

He moved his neck again.

Six

Kristi smiled sleepily as she felt Dev brush the back of her neck. The dashing, debonair Dev was necking with her! But somehow she didn't feel threatened by his casual advance. The warmth of the sun was reassuring, as were the musical calls of the swans on the lake. And the strong arms that held her. She bent her head, arching her neck, offering him better access.

Dev took advantage of her offer, feathering kiss after kiss against the wisps of hair which clung to the nape of her neck. Hers was such a long, graceful neck, but so vulnerable. And she had such luxurious hair. So soft and silky, smelling of roses.

Dreamily Kristi wondered if she should put a stop to Dev's foolishness. And to hers. She was such a silly goose to let him kiss her, but she was enjoying it so much. His lips sent shivers through her body, shivers of delight and excitement. Shivers which made her want to tell Dev to stop, but also made her want more.

Dev told himself he should stop. Instead, he turned Kristi in his arms, seeking the hollow of her collarbone with his lips. The open neck of her shirt lured him on. Nuzzling the shirt aside, he lay his cheek against her chest. Her skin was like satin, so tender beneath his scratchy whiskers. With a murmured apology he turned his head and sought her with his lips. Slowly he continued his quest, loving every second of it, all the while wondering when Kristi was going to call a halt. At the entrance to the enticing valley between her breasts, he paused, his nerves singing with anticipation.

Would she allow him to chart the territory that had beckoned all morning?

As Dev's lips moved lower and lower, Kristi's awareness of his lips—and her body—rose higher and higher. Just the warmth of his breath against her skin was enough to toast her toes, while his lips created a fire of their own. And his whiskers prickled. Prickled and tickled and tormented secret places deep inside her. Places she never knew existed.

But Dev knew they existed, came the warning voice from the cautious place inside Kristi. Hadn't he admitted that the women in Washington followed him around like a gaggle of geese.

Well, this silly goose wasn't about to join his flock.

"Don't," she whispered, pulling out of his arms to sit with her knees drawn up to her chest.

Dev gazed at Kristi in bemusement. Dammit all anyway, he thought in disgust. Here he'd just decided he needed to win her trust, and then he'd gotten carried away. What the hell was the matter with him, anyway?

"Sorry about that, Kristi," he said, giving her a contrite smile. "I didn't mean to ruffle your feathers."

"I'm not a bird," she said indignantly.

He glanced at the lake then back at Kristi. "And even if you were one of those swans out there, I've done nothing to win your trust, have I?"

The regret in his voice seeped into her, easing the tension in the pit of her stomach, and she offered an apology of her own. "It wasn't all your fault."

"I have the feeling I'm fighting ghosts," he said, his

green eyes probing Kristi's. "You've been hurt, haven't you?"

"Let's just say I've learned to be leary of men who come around camp."

"Who was he, Kristi?"

For a moment Kristi hesitated. Why should she tell Dev about her love life? But there was something about him, possibly his air of expectant waiting, that made her want to tell him. Besides, he deserved an explanation for the way she was acting.

"Fergus McIntyre," she said, then wiggled her nose as if the name had produced a rotten smell. "He was a university professor from Minnesota. He arrived in camp one summer when Dad was away on a speaking engagement. I was twenty and shy, and Fergus was handsome and charming and knew his way around women." She shook her head as Dev started to say something, and a self-mocking smile touched her lips as she continued. "While I was dreaming about marriage and a life of working together, he was busy picking my brains for the research results he needed to obtain tenure. I willingly gave him the information. And I probably would've given him more, but Dad came back in the nick of time—as the old melodrama goes."

"And now I've arrived on the scene, and you're not sure whether I'm a hero or a villain in the play," Dev said, wondering if this was the reason she distrusted him so much. "Well, you can be certain of one thing, Kristi. I would never use you."

Kristi stared at Dev, trying to decide whether she should believe him or not. "Funny. Fergus said the same thing."

"You think I'm trying to seduce you into coming to work for me?"

"Why else would you be kissing me?"

He opened his mouth, then closed it again. Why was he kissing her? If he searched deep inside and found the truth, he'd be running for the south pole, and if he told her, she'd be running in the opposite direction.

"Because you're a beautiful woman, and I'm a hot-blooded man," he said, settling on the most superficial and therefore less disturbing reason that came to mind.

The knowledge that her blood was just as hot flushed her cheeks. "Tell me another one," she said, taking refuge in flippancy.

Because every time I look into your big blue eyes, I'm lost."

He gave her a slow, sexy smile that made her blood boil, then a broad wink that cooled things and put them in perspective. Dev was teasing!

She chuckled, feeling lighthearted and relaxed for the first time since she'd remembered his Washington women. "Spare me the rest."

Dev gazed at her thoughtfully. "Outside of a certain good-for-nothing weasel you haven't had much experience around men, have you, Kristi?"

She hid her face against her knees for a moment then raised her head and met his gaze. "No, I haven't. Twenty-six and barely been kissed. That's me."

"What's the matter with the men in Alaska? Are they all blind?" he asked, the expression in his eyes matching his appreciative smile.

The smile did wonders for her ego, making her feel as if she were the most beautiful woman in the world, and suddenly Kristi felt more confident about herself than she'd ever felt before. "I don't see many men when I'm in the field, and I had to work part-time to put myself through college. Besides, the college crowd seemed too young. Don't get me wrong. I have lots of friends but no man I'd want to make a commitment to."

"I can see how living close to nature would give you a different outlook on what's important in life. You take mating as seriously as those swans, don't you?"

Kristi nodded, unable to look away from his soul-searching eyes. It was absolutely uncanny the way Dev could read her innermost thoughts.

"And so do I," he continued softly. "I don't believe in one-night stands or casual relationships."

"But you admitted that you make the gossip column regularly."

"That's all it is. Gossip. I need to be seen about town, and the press needs to make copy."

For some reason she believed him. But how many of his dates harbored secret thoughts of hooking him? She couldn't blame them. He'd be a trophy catch. "You can't have reached the ripe old age of thirty without having been seriously involved with someone," she said, releasing the grip on her knees and flexing her fingers.

"I thought you decided I didn't have a serious bone in my body," he said in an attempt to sidetrack her.

"Stop dragging your wing, Dev. It's your turn to level."

She was right, Dev admitted. After all, she had just shared her heartache with him, the least he could do was tell her about his.

"I met Brenda the first year of college, and we quickly became a twosome," he said quietly. "We had the same interests, the same idealistic view of what the world should be like, and together we took on any worthwhile cause that came along. I cared about her, and I thought we'd eventually get married and raise a bunch of little crusaders . . . but she cared more about her cause than she did about me. She went off to Ethiopia to be a missionary doctor. And I hurt Brenda, too, because I wouldn't go with her."

He gave Kristi a self-conscious smile as he realized she was the first person he'd ever told about Brenda. What was there about Kristi, he wondered, that made him willing to bare his soul?

Kristi returned his smile and reached out to touch

his hand. "Losing her that way must have left a big hole in your life."

"It left me with a lot of questions," he said, grateful for Kristi's understanding. "About commitment, dedication, what I believed in. It took a while, but I sorted it out."

She squeezed his hand. "And?"

He stared at their hands and debated whether to tell the truth or make a joke. Dammit all to hell, he was no better than Fergus. He wouldn't blame Kristi for thinking he was using her.

Slowly he raised his head and looked her square in the eye. "And I decided that I would never again become personally involved with a woman who is dedicated to a cause. I'm a crusader, Kristi. I'll be a crusader till my dying day, and I need a wife who will work along beside me, not go chasing off on her own crusade."

Kristi's eyes grew wary as the ramifications of his words hit home. Releasing his hand, she gripped her knees again. "You know how strongly I feel about birds."

He nodded. "And I admire you for your dedication to them. It's the reason I want you to work for the commission. However, it's also the reason I keep telling myself that I shouldn't be kissing you, shouldn't be wanting you, shouldn't be . . ." He gave her a lopsided smile.

Trying to ignore his smile was like trying to ignore the northern lights, and Kristi had to summon every ounce of willpower to force herself to her feet. Once upright, she placed her hands on her hips and took a deep breath. "Then why do you keep kissing me?"

His expression became even more sheepish, even more endearing as he rose to stand beside her. "Damn if I know, Kristi. One minute I'm warning myself that you're a dangerous woman, and the next minute I'm kissing you."

The confusion in his voice tugged at her heartstrings, making her laugh despite her reservations. "You definitely have a problem."

He gave a brief laugh, then sobered abruptly. "My main problem is that I don't want to hurt you, Kristi, the way I hurt Brenda."

"Don't worry. I can take care of myself."

Suddenly he wanted to shake the self-confidence she wore like a shield. He leaned closer. "You're sure about that?"

"Yes." All she'd have to do was keep reminding herself that he was a King.

His head bent lower. "Very sure?"

"Yes," she whispered.

His lips brushed hers.

"I'm not so sure," she breathed against them.

Slowly he lifted his head and gazed earnestly into her eyes. "Well, I'm absolutely positively certain about one thing. I won't kiss you again unless you ask me to." He gave her a quick hug. "But be warned. I was raised by a mother who believes in hugs, and I've just realized how much I miss them."

Kristi lay in her sleeping bag at the campsite, listening for the sound that had wakened her. Had it been Dev's snoring or something else?

Beside her, Rex cocked his head and whimpered, and then there was silence again. Kristi listened to the silence, wishing it was broken by Dev's snores. At least they were normal.

Suddenly the husky growled and crawled to the tent door. Something was definitely wrong, Kristi realized, quickly sliding out of the sleeping bag.

A low moan split the night air, raising the hairs on the back of her neck. Dev must be in pain, she thought, as she slipped into her moccasins. She barely managed to unzip the mosquito netting before Rex tore out into the night, growling and barking.

"Rex, come back here," she yelled, grabbing the shotgun on the way out the door.

Pumping a shell into the chamber, she joined the hackled dog who was barking at the pingo. Together they stalked around the mound and confronted a startled wolverine, which took one look at them and fled.

Dev, dressed in sweatpants and moccasins and carrying the harpoon, crawled out of his tent to see an animal disappear into the gloom. He hobbled forward, then stopped as Kristi appeared from behind the pingo with Rex trotting at her side.

Feeling totally useless, Dev leaned on the harpoon and lifted his right foot off the ground. "Guess I wasn't needed. You seem to have everything under control."

"A woman should be able to protect herself against unwelcome guests," she said as she came to a stop in front of him.

One good look at Kristi's formfitting white long johns banished Dev's disappointment. "Well, honey, you sure need protection in that outfit," he drawled, then gave a long, low whistle.

That was a wolf whistle if she'd ever heard one, Kristi thought, and glanced down at her long johns, wondering if he were making fun of her. "What did you expect, anyway? I'm just a backwoods gal."

"Don't get me wrong. On you, they look downright fetching." The way they hugged the swell of her breasts and the nipped-in curve of her waist was the sexiest thing he'd ever seen, and he just wished his foot wasn't throbbing like the very devil so he could enjoy the view.

Embarrassed by his admiring gaze, Kristi turned away, then stopped abruptly. The fact that he was making like a stork reminded her of the moan she'd heard earlier. It was a sure bet the wolverine hadn't moaned. "Is your foot hurting?"

"It's all right," he muttered, not wanting to bother

her again. She'd done enough already, more than enough. Rex padded over, and Dev held perfectly still while the dog sniffed his foot then turned his head toward Kristi and whined.

"Just the same, I think I'd better take a look." Cradling the gun in the crook of her arm, she reached out to help Dev into his tent, then took one look at his naked chest and changed her mind. "Go put on your coat and I'll meet you in the kitchen," she ordered, turning abruptly toward her own tent.

Armed with a parka shell over her long johns, a lantern, and first-aid kit, she felt brave enough to face Dev. He had put on his bomber jacket and was sitting on his box with his injured foot propped on another and Rex's head propped on his knee.

"You're fussing over nothing," he said, knowing he lied but wishing it were true.

She knelt beside him, lifted his foot onto her lap, and began peeling off the bandages. "We'll see."

The light from the lantern confirmed her fears. The flesh around the wound was red and puffy. She touched it with a gentle finger. It was also hot. Raising her head, she studied Dev carefully. His eyes were bright, and she suspected he was running a fever despite the cold night air.

"This looks bad, Tenderfoot. I'll have to draw out the infection." Replacing his foot on the box, Kristi strode quickly around the campsite, picking up a can of kerosene and a clean bucket. "I admit this is a little unorthodox," she said, as the liquid gurgled into the bucket. "But I've seen it work before."

"I hope you don't intend to light a match," he said, trying to lighten the mood.

Kneeling beside him once more, Kristi pulled up the bottom of his pants until the cuff fit snugly around his muscular leg. As she lifted his leg, the feel of his hair-roughened skin distracted her for a moment, then she quickly shoved his foot into the bucket.

Dev just managed to stifle a gasp as the kerosene bit into the wound. Rex whined and Dev buried his free hand into his thick coat, thankful for something to hold on to.

"I wish I could offer you a good stiff drink," she said as she rose to her feet.

"I'd settle for a hug," he said wistfully.

Kristi stared down at Dev, wondering if she dare give him a hug. For some unknown reason she longed to hug him . . . longed to sit beside him and touch him . . . and it wasn't just because she missed having someone to touch, she knew.

He gave her a coaxing smile. "No need to worry about my having my way with you. I couldn't. Not with a killer dog on my lap and one foot in the bucket."

She laughed at his sally, relaxing for the first time since she'd heard his moan. He was right, she could easily escape if he tried something funny. And he wasn't going to do that. Hadn't he told her that he didn't want to become involved with her. Hadn't he promised he wouldn't even kiss her unless she asked. And she wasn't about to ask, was she?

As she pulled up the campstool and sat down beside him, he slipped his arm around her back and gave her a grateful hug. After a moment she slid her arm around him and hugged him back. He sighed in contentment, caught the scent of roses, and sighed again. Roses reminded him of home.

"Please talk to me, Kristi," he said, knowing she was the real reason he was thinking of home.

Kristi gave a little start of surprise as she realized she was cuddled up against Dev. What was there about him that made her feel so safe in his arms, when she really should be keeping her distance? She tired to pull away but he held her, and she relaxed again, deciding it was too much trouble to move.

"For heaven's sake, I spent the whole evening talking to you," she murmured. "I don't know what got into me. I normally don't say more than two sentences at a time, and I went on for hours about my birds." Except when her gaze had drifted to Dev's and all coherent thought had taken wing.

"And I enjoyed every minute of it," he said, his voice husky with suppressed emotion. "In fact I've been happier during the last two days than I've been for a long time. It's kind of hard to explain the feeling, but it's almost like being back home with my family. When I was growing up, the family shared everything—the work, the laughter, the tears—the same things you and I have been sharing. I guess I must miss them." He smiled as he felt Kristi's hand rubbing the back of his jacket, almost as if she were trying to comfort him, and he gave her a little hug as he realized that she, too, probably needed comforting. "You must miss your father."

Suddenly Kristi realized just how much she did miss having her father around camp. That was why she'd enjoyed talking to Dev so much, she decided. Rex provided company, but it was fun to have someone who would converse, laugh at her jokes, or even tease her. So she'd savor the moments now, she decided, and treasure them later when she was alone once more.

"You're right, I do miss him," she said, snuggling closer to Dev even as she told herself she shouldn't. "He's the talker in the family. He has a way with words that completely mesmerizes a crowd. I've always admired his ability to stand up in front of a roomful of people and hold their interest—more than that, to make them believe in what he's saying."

Dev smiled to himself, liking the way she always spoke so highly of her father almost as much as he liked the feel of her soft body against his. "Haven't you made any of the presentations at the environmental hearings or on the lecture circuit?" he asked.

"Only once, and that was enough."

Dev thought he felt her shiver slightly, so he

hugged her again. He knew what it was like to live under the iron hand of his father and wondered if Kristi was experiencing the same problem. "Kristi, does your father deliberately keep you in the background?"

She laughed softly. "For heaven's sake, no. In fact, he's been after me to start making speeches."

"Then why don't you?" he asked, puzzled.

"I'm perfectly happy doing what I do best, gathering facts and writing the speeches. I'll leave the speaking to someone else, thank you very much."

He felt her start to pull away and tightened his arms around her. "Anyway, enough about that," he said hastily, not wanting to spoil what was turning out to be a very pleasurable experience, now that his foot had stopped aching. "Tell me about your mother. You've never mentioned her."

Kristi knew she should make the effort to sit up straight, to draw away her chair, to put some distance between herself and Dev, but it was easier to talk when she was in the comfort of his arms.

"Mom left Alaska when I was ten. My parents should never have gotten married, but they thought their love would overcome their differences." She swallowed hard, trying to ease the tightness that gripped her throat every time she talked about her mother. "Mom was from California and she hated the North, especially the winters," Kristi continued, her voice still husky. "My earliest memories are of her crying. She tried to stay with us, but she finally had to leave. And Father, who was afraid she'd get so depressed she'd commit suicide, let her go. She's always kept in touch, but she's never come back north."

Dev's heart ached for Kristi, although he could only guess at the hurt she had felt when her mother had left. "Have you ever visited her?"

"Once, when we were giving a lecture in Florida. She came with her new husband and family, and

Dad encouraged me to spend the weekend with them. Later I realized how much it cost him to let me go with her; he was afraid he would lose me too. Of course there's no chance of that ever happening. I love Alaska, and I'd react the same way my mother did if I had to spend the rest of my life somewhere else."

Oh, Lord, Dev thought, hearing a warning in Kristi's story. Even if he did manage to convince her to come work with him, she had just told him in no uncertain terms that she wouldn't stay for long.

"Mom can't understand how I feel," Kristi continued sadly. "She still keeps trying to convince me to move south, mainly, I think because she's afraid for my safety."

"She has every reason to be afraid. I don't like your being out here by yourself, and we're not even related."

The concern in his voice sent a flicker of forboding through Kristi, and with a sigh of resignation she straightened her spine and moved away from him. "This morning I thought it was kind of nice that you were worrying about me, but it could become a real bore," she warned him.

"Sorry," Dev said. "I'll try to do better. The last thing I'd want is to become a bore."

She gave a soft little laugh. "There's little chance of that happening. One way or another, you've kept me busier than a mother hen with a dozen chicks since you've arrived."

He gently squeezed her shoulder, then released it to take her hand. "I know, and my mother would have me horsewhipped because I haven't thanked you for everything you've done for me."

His solemn eyes never left hers as he slowly raised her hand to his lips. "Thank you for taking me in out of the cold and giving me a place to stay," he said, brushing a kiss against the back of her hand.

Her heart gave a little pitter-patter of pleasure,

then a little flip when he turned her hand over and kissed her wrist.

"And thank you for sewing up my foot this morning," he said as he lifted his head slightly then pressed another kiss into her palm. "Finally, thank you, for all the TLC you gave me tonight." He raised his head and smiled into her startled eyes. "These kisses are poor substitutes for the ones I'd really like to give you, but I'm afraid they'll have to do."

"Th-they'll d-do just fine," Kristi whispered breathlessly, but later as she lay in her sleeping bag once more, she admitted that she'd much rather have had a real kiss. . . .

And much later Kristi was still awake, fretting about her primitive first-aid methods. The last thing she needed was for Dev to get blood poisoning. Dev would have to go to the hospital today. If he couldn't fly his plane, she'd take him.

However, this time she didn't want him to go.

Dev accepted the mug of coffee with a sleepy smile and a soft nuzzle against her neck, and sank onto the box. Kristi stared at him, feeling as soppy as the sourdough she was mixing, then stiffened her resolve. "You have to go."

Green eyes, no longer sleepy, swept up to meet blue ones. "I thought we'd been through this before."

"I should've insisted you go to the hospital yesterday. Now your foot is infected, and you need antibiotics and better medical treatment than I can give you."

"Whoa, whoa. It's too early in the morning to start pecking at me," he said, reaching down to pat Rex, who had sprawled on top of his good foot.

"Well, I'm worried about you." She spooned the pancake mixture into the hot grease.

"You're worried about a King? Maybe I'm making progress."

The smile that creased his cheeks almost took her breath away.

He gave an exaggerated sigh. "And now I'm going to blow it. My foot is much better."

She stared at him in disbelief. "What?"

"The kerosene seems to have done the trick. I looked and there's no infection."

"I don't believe you."

"You can check it out if you want, but let's wait until after breakfast. The smell of that bacon is mouth watering."

Canned bacon was expensive, and Kristi had decided to open one in honor of her guest's last day. Now he was telling her there was no reason to send him away, she thought, torn between exasperation and a vague sense of relief. At the moment she knew only one thing for certain: There was no one else she'd rather share her precious bacon with than this handsome tenderfoot.

He was right about his foot, she acknowledged an hour later after inspecting his wound. It was on the mend. She rebandaged it, wondering again why she was feeling so relieved.

"I can stay?" Dev asked hopefully.

She raised her eyes to meet his. "Yes, you can stay until the owlet flies," she said, and finally admitted why the world seemed suddenly brighter. She'd have Dev around camp for a few more days.

Seven

Thank goodness the owls were still there, Dev thought, early Thursday morning as he bellied up to the brow of the hill and looked at the gravesite. The female was keeping tabs on her scurrying chick, and the smaller, whiter male was hunting lemming to feed his family.

Turning his head, Dev covertly studied Kristi, who was stretched out beside him. He'd been surprised and dismayed when she'd suggested they check out the owls. Had she gotten tired of his company? Or worse yet, had she gotten so fed up with him asking her to work for him that she'd finally decided to send him packing?

He didn't want to leave, but leave he must—in just three short days. And unless a miracle happened, Kristi wouldn't be coming with him. He had used every argument he could think of to persuade her, and every ounce of his charm, to no avail. To his shame, he'd even considered—for a few weak moments—to use sex. But no way did he want it rumored around town that Kristi had slept her way into the job . . . if she ever agreed to take it.

He gazed at her, longing for her to turn to him and tell him she'd changed her mind. Lord, how he'd miss her if she didn't come south. She had seeped into his lifeblood until even the thought of leaving her created an emptiness inside him as vast as this empty land.

She turned to him and smiled. He smiled back, his eyes roving over her face, resting on her lips as he wondered what she'd do if he kissed her. The fact that he hadn't kissed her again should have won him a Congressional Medal of honor. If she smiled at him once more, he'd . . . no, he wouldn't. He didn't even dare think about kissing her, because after one kiss, he'd throw honor to the wind and make love to her.

Kristi stared at Dev, wishing he would kiss her. The wish had been simmering in her for days, alternately dampened by Dev's restraint and fueled by all the nesting and nurturing that was going on around her. Before, she'd just made observations. Now the actions of the birds were making her very aware of her own body and of her own needs.

Admit it, she admonished herself. The birds weren't affecting her. Dev was.

His arm felt so solid beneath her hand, and he smelled so manly—of warm leather and spice—that it made her mouth water. Slowly she trailed her fingers up the leather sleeve to his shoulder. Wistful eyes followed the progress of her hand, then lifted to his face. She'd been dying to stroke him all morning, ever since she'd watched him shave.

He caught his breath, and then he smiled again. The smile was her downfall, and giving in to the urge, she lifted her hand to explore the laughter crease. His skin felt smooth and taut beneath her fingertips, and she brushed it again and again, marveling at how much pleasure she derived from the simple act of touching Dev. Her eyes sought his lips—moist, full, oh-so-kissable lips—and she grew all warm inside as she remembered how they had felt against hers.

A plaintive whistling sound shattered the moment,

and Kristi saw her surprise mirrored in Dev's eyes. Had she cried out in yearning? Or had he? The cry came again—up from the lake—bringing with a shiver of premonition that reached them both at the same time. Something was wrong with one of the swans.

Kristi lowered her hand to grip Dev's arm, and they slid quietly away from the brow of the hill.

"What's the matter?" he whispered, as they stood up to study the lake.

Kristi pointed to the pebbled shore at the bottom of the hill. "Something's happened to the pen."

The swan, awkward at the best of times when out of the water, was so weak, she could barely waddle along the beach. Nearby swam the male and five brownish-gray cygnets.

"Whatever is wrong with her hasn't affected the cob or the young," Kristi said, remembering there were five the last time she'd counted the hatch.

The cob glided back and forth in quick passes along the shore, obviously distressed. "But he sure is upset," Dev said, knowing he'd feel the same way if something were wrong with Kristi.

"No wonder. They mate for life." Kristi began creeping slowly down the hill with Dev at her side. "I heard a story once about a pen being caught in the ice on the lower Detroit River. She was rescued by conservation officers and nursed back to health, and all the while her mate waited forlornly until she was well enough to join him again."

Dev's heart turned over in a slow loop and seemed to bottom out somewhere very deep inside. Devotion of that magnitude was rare, even in humans. No, he was wrong about that. He knew a few women—the Duchess and his mother—whose devotion to their husbands would rival the swans. Kristi's devotion, however, would be tempered by her love for her birds.

Reaching the beach, they came to a halt a few

yards away from the swan. "Look," Kristi said softly as the pen turned to face them and half raised her wings. "There's the problem."

Dangling from the swan's black beak were five empty rings of a six-pack. The sixth plastic ring was clamped high up around her beak. "Good Lord, she's starving to death," Dev said, feeling sick with anger. "What maniac would leave something like that lying around?"

"Probably a fisherman or someone exploring for oil. Most people toss plastic away, thinking it will magically disappear. But it doesn't. Especially up here."

"Can we do something to help her?"

"We can try," Kristi said, thankful for Dev's assistance. "If you'll distract her, I'll sneak up from behind and subdue her. Then we'll see if we can pull that thing off. And it would help if I could use your jacket."

Without question, Dev shrugged off his bomber jacket and handed it to Kristi. Slowly he approached the pen, trying not to frighten her. The bird struck out at him feebly with her beak, then collapsed in a squat. At that moment Kristi dropped the jacket over the swan's back and grasped the top of her long neck. Crooning softly to the immobilized pen, Kristi tugged at the plastic. It wouldn't budge.

"Are you carrying a knife?" she asked Dev.

"No."

"There's one in my back pocket."

After digging the knife out of Kristi's pocket—an experience he wished he had more time to enjoy—he moved around the the swan's head. The pen stared at him with luminous brown eyes, the yellow feathers at the corners looking ever so much like golden teardrops.

"Hurry," Kristi urged as the male came hissing out of the water.

Careful despite his haste, Dev slid the blade under

the plastic ring and began sawing. The cob hit him broadside with angry wings and a brutal beak. Dev rocked forward under the attack, grateful the knife bit into his thumb and not the pen. Bracing himself for another onslaught, he continued sawing. The ring broke just as the male hit him again. Turning, he waved his arms at the hissing swan, trying to distract him. The cob charged, and Dev, hampered by his still healing foot, hobbled down the beach, barely keeping clear of the out-thrust beak.

Releasing the pen, Kristi herded her toward the lake with Dev's jacket. "You can stop running, Tenderfoot," she called, chest aching with the need to laugh. The sight of Dev being chased by the angry swan tickled her funny bone.

It also warmed her heart. And if she wasn't careful, she'd do something foolish, like fall in love with the dear tenderfoot.

She held Dev's jacket against her breasts as she watched him shoo the male toward the lake. With a final hiss and thrust of his beak, the cob swaggered into the water, lord of his domain.

Snapping the blade closed, Dev shoved his left hand, the knife, and the plastic rings into the pocket of his jeans, leaving them there. Head down, he picked his way toward Kristi, hopping and limping over the sharp stones. As he reached her the flutelike cries of the swans drew their attention. The cob was swimming toward the pen, head up and wings raised. Opening her wings, she reared up and welcomed the conquering hero. Their long necks weaved back and forth—brushing, touching, as if assuring each other that all was well and that each was loved.

Lord but he envied that cob, Dev thought. Cocking his head, he smiled at Kristi.

Kristi's heart melted completely as she saw his slow, sweet smile. Every nerve ending quivered with the urge to open her arms, and she gripped his jacket tightly with both hands. If he said one word, or touched her, she would throw her arms around him.

The silence sizzled between them, and finally Dev turned his attention to the lake. "Do you think she'll make it?" he asked as the pen finished preening and gave herself a vigorous shake which ended in a twitch of her tail feathers.

"I think so."

Dev glanced back at Kristi, his eyes growing tender as he remembered her story about the swans. "I'm glad. He was going to be awfully lonely without her."

"There aren't many birds that remain faithful to their mates. That's why I love the swans," she said. "And they both help in raising the young."

"Doesn't watching all this nesting day after day give you the urge to have a nest and young ones of your own?"

"I admit there have been moments." Especially these past four days, she thought, lowering her gaze quickly so he couldn't guess what she was thinking. Suddenly she realized she'd been caressing his jacket, almost as if she'd been caressing a lover. And she knew that lover was Dev. Startled she looked up to find his attention focused on her fingers. "But my work is important too," she added hastily.

Dev stared at Kristi's fingers, wishing she was caressing him instead of the jacket. The mere brush of her fingers against his cheek earlier had sent the blood surging through him. What would it be like if she stroked his chest, his thigh, his—

The wish was mirrored in his eyes when he raised them to meet hers. The blatant need was too much and, clasping the coat against her body, Kristi began walking down the beach toward the plane.

Dev limped beside her, his left fist clenched around the plastic rings as he fought to control the gut-gripping desire to make love to Kristi right on the spot.

"Are you going to let your birds prevent you from having a husband and a family?" he asked, thinking it would be a shame if Kristi wasted all her nurturing instincts on her birds.

Kristi braved a quick glance at Dev, then looked out at the lake. "I'm like the Tundra Swans. If I ever get married, it will be till death do us part."

"I feel the same way," he said, his soft voice full of conviction. "I believe that when souls find their mates, the bond lasts forever, even after death."

She gazed at Dev with wide eyes as his words whispered into her soul. He was such a beautiful man, she thought, both inside and out, and he had a way of saying things that made her feel like crying. "Then you'll understand why I can't marry someone who'd try to change me," she said, wishing she had met Dev in another time, another place where their souls would have had a chance of belonging together. "I'd be miserable if my wings were clipped, and I'd make life so miserable for my husband, we'd wind up hating each other."

"But if you found the right man that wouldn't happen," Dev said, ignoring the nagging voice that told him such a man didn't exist.

"What man would let his wife fly off to watch birds all summer?"

He took a deep breath and released it in a long sigh. "You have a point there," he admitted. "If we were married, I sure as hell wouldn't want you to go north every year." He'd be worried spitless that something would happen to her. . . . like it had happened to his grandfather.

Kristi stared at Dev, disappointed that he had agreed with her, but not in the least bit surprised. He had warned her they wouldn't have a future together, and his attitude was just one more reason why things would never work between them.

With a sigh of resignation she started to hand him the bomber jacket, then clutched it under her arm as she remembered something else. "I'd better see how much damage the swan did to your back. Turn around."

"It's nothing," he said, obeying her order.

She pulled up his green cable-knit sweater. "You always say that," she muttered, her fingertips tingling from their contact with his skin.

"And you're always taking off my clothes."

Heat rushed through her veins at his words, quickly followed by a shiver as she caught sight of the angry red flesh, already turning purple. She laughed, the sound catching in her throat and coming out breathlessly. "I can't help it. You're an accident looking for a place to happen. How do you ever manage at home?"

"You won't believe this, but nothing like this ever happens to me at home."

She stared at the bruise, feeling an unaccountable urge to kiss it. "Then maybe you'd better fly back to the safe south," she said, not really meaning it this time.

"I don't want to go," he said quietly, admitting what he'd been thinking all day.

And she didn't want him to go either, Kristi admitted silently.

Hastily, she pulled down his sweater. "Well, I guess you'll survive this brush with nature." She held out his jacket. "Here, put this on. You'll get cold."

Throwing back his head, he laughed. Sheepishly, she joined in, but her laughter died when she caught sight of his left hand as it emerged from the sleeve.

"You cut yourself."

"It's just a scratch." He held up his thumb for her inspection. "All it needs is a kiss to make it better."

Without stopping to think, she touched her lips to his thumb. The taste of blood and his startled gasp made her realize what she'd done. Drawing back, she stared at him in confusion. "The lengths you go to to get a kiss," she said, as her heart began misbehaving again, skipping a beat then fluttering wildly.

Dev's hand cradled her cheek. "I've been wanting to kiss you for days," he said, his voice husky with raw, aching need. "But do you want me to kiss you?"

She met his gaze and slowly nodded her head. "Yes, Dev. Please."

With a slight grin of triumph he lowered his head and took captive her lips. The triumph lasted for half a heartbeat until she responded. Then he, too, was captive.

The ground heaved beneath his feet, and he wrapped his arms around her and held on for dear life. It was as though the heat from the kiss had melted right down to the permafrost, turning the land into molasses. Just like his insides, Dev thought wildly. They'd been aching with need for days, and now that she'd finally kissed him the ache was almost overwhelming.

Her tongue teased his lips, and when he opened his mouth, she eagerly slipped it inside, thrusting deeply. He heard a groan and knew it had come from him. Cupping her bottom in the palms of his hands, he tilted her up to meet his pelvis.

Shocked by the discovery of his arousal, Kristi drew back slightly. He refused to let her go, swaying against her slowly, suggestively while his tongue showed her exactly what he wanted to do to her. A quivering feeling began deep inside, spreading wider and wider with each brush of his pelvis, each thrust of his tongue. Her knees trembled as she acknowledged the feeling as desire. There was nothing on this earth she'd rather do than make love to Dev.

Dev felt her body tremble, and a wave of longing swept through him. Not only did his body ache for her, his soul yearned for her, and his heart longed to soar to the heavens with her.

Their lips still clinging, they sank to the ground. She lay back against the soft tundra, drawing him down to cover her. Sun-warmed minutes passed filled with murmurs and gasps and the sweet scent of crushed flowers.

Bracing his weight on his arm, Dev raised up slightly and gazed down at Kristi. His eyes grew softer as he noticed the white-gold flowers that pillowed her white-gold head. "You're so beautiful, Kristi." He touched her kiss-swollen lips. "So passionate."

"Oh, Dev," she said, burying her hands in his thick hair.

With a low growl he lowered his head to forge a trail of hot kisses down her throat into the opening of her shirt. Suddenly he wanted to do more than savor her beauty with his lips.

"I want to see you," he said softly, nuzzling her breasts before raising his head to seek her permission.

He found it in her dazzling eyes and her trembling smile. Slowly, his eyes never leaving hers, he began unbuttoning her shirt. Pulling it free of the waistband, he slipped his hands into the opening and peeled it back.

Then, and only then, did he look at her, his eyes growing wide in appreciation, then heavy lidded with desire. "You're absolutely beautiful."

Kristi reveled in the knowledge that Dev wanted her. And she wanted him. Her breasts throbbed and her nipples ached, longing for his touch, his kiss. She had never felt so sexy, so desirable, so very much a woman.

Leisurely he trailed his index finger down the curve of her breast, then up again to circle the rosy nipple. He nearly drove her crazy. She wanted to press his hand to her breast and end her torment, but she didn't want to miss anything. Arching her back, she brought her other breast to his attention.

"So downy soft," he murmured as he began stroking the neglected breast as well.

She gasped, wetting her lips, which had suddenly gone dry, while everything within her was focused on his fingertips touching her.

"So ivory-white," he said, his voice so deep and sexy that it sent chills of longing down her spine. "And I just have to taste you."

The pressure of his lips on her aching nipple caused a wave of desire to pulse through her. She whimpered, wanting him to stop but also wanting more.

Dev moved to her other breast, flicking the nipple with his tongue before closing his mouth over it. "So heavenly sweet," he whispered against her swollen, needy flesh.

Unable to hold still any longer, Kristi began moving, seeking his legs with hers, trying to entice him to cover her body with his. His lips covered hers as he heeded the call, snuggling into the cradle of her thighs as if he belonged.

She moaned as his hardness pressed against her, wishing there were no barriers between them, wishing she could feel his flesh against hers, his flesh in hers. With impatient hands, she found his belt buckle and loosened it.

"Love me, Dev, please love me," she begged, as she slipped her hand inside his jeans to capture him.

The touch of her hands brought with them the promise of heaven. . . . and the threat of hell. He raised his head and gazed down at her, his eyes glazed with passion. "Kristi, sweetheart. We have to stop."

Eight

Kristi pulled her hands away and stared at Dev in confusion. "Did I do something wrong?" she asked, feeling frustrated and bewildered and cheated, and wishing above all that she wasn't so inexperienced when it came to pleasing a man.

His shoulders heaved as he sucked in one deep breath and a second, then slowly, very carefully, he lifted his body off hers and lay at her side. "It isn't you, Kristi. It's me." Reaching out with trembling fingers, he touched her cheek tenderly, regretfully. "Here I've been trying to find a way protect you, and the only thing you need protection from is me."

"What are you talking about?" she asked, more confused than ever.

"I'm still hanging on to the hope that you'll come work for me, Kristi, and I don't want anyone on the Hill intimating that I gave you the job because you've slept with me."

"They wouldn't dare!" she said indignantly. "I'm as well qualified for the job as anyone else you could find."

"I know that, and you know that." He gave her a crooked smile. "But there's a certain way a man looks at a woman after he's made love to her, and I'm not very good at hiding my feelings. I'm afraid we'd be a news item as soon as we hit town."

He was already looking at her in a certain way, and they hadn't even made love, Kristi thought in bemusement.

Emotions churned inside, and she closed her eyes tightly, afraid they would spill over in tears. Tears of frustration and disappointment that Dev had called a halt to their lovemaking; tears of tenderness and . . . love? . . . because Dev had been more concerned about her reputation than his own needs. Dear, devilish Dev, trying to be a true gentleman, even if it was going to kill him.

He continued to stroke her cheek in silence, but she could feel his eyes compelling her to look at him. When she finally did, she was composed enough to say, "Well, you won't have to worry about sharing the scandal sheets with me, because I'm certainly not going to work for you."

He gave her a long, considered look. "So, does that mean you want to make love with me?"

"No way," she whispered breathlessly, wondering in her heart of hearts if she'd lied.

He gave her a little hug, then pulled her closer to his chest. "It's probably for the best. I'm not carrying anything to protect you, and I don't want to risk making you pregnant."

After a moment, she laughed softly. "I think you've just proven you aren't a playboy."

He sighed. "And I wasn't a Boy Scout either."

They lay in silence while he gently threaded his fingers through her hair, and the assurance crept into Kristi's mind that Dev wasn't one bit like Fergus. He would never use her. Finally she spoke, her voice a mere whisper. "I'm on the pill."

He stiffened, then relaxed. "Trust you to have everything under control. As usual."

"It's not what you think. I mean, it's not as though I'm expecting to jump into the sack with every man who flies into camp. It's just that . . ." She rubbed her forehead against his sweater. "Oh, never mind."

He drew away slightly and smiled at her. When she wouldn't look at him, he crooked a finger under her chin and raised her head. He touched her swollen bottom lip with his thumb. "I'm glad you are, Kristi, for whatever reason."

"I take them to control cramps," she admitted shyly, wondering why she was revealing all these intimate secrets to Dev. "Otherwise they're so bad, I have to spend a couple of days in bed."

Dev continued to smile at her as he brushed her lip again and again. For one weak moment he was tempted to say to hell with the job, honor, and everything else he held dear, and make love to Kristi. But if he did, he wouldn't be able to look his mother in the eye again. Madre King had raised her boys to respect and honor women, and he would do no less than honor Kristi. Lowering his head, he placed a lingering kiss on her lips, then sat up beside her.

Kristi stared up at Dev, wishing with the recklessly wanting part of her mind that he would make love to her, while the cautious part demanded to know if she *really* was ready to make love with him. His warm body no longer protected her from the wind, and the touch of the cool air against her breasts made her realize just how close she'd come to being completely intimate with a man who had warned her that he would never let her into his life. Still watching him— but this time from beneath the shelter of her thick lashes—she reached for her shirt with trembling hands.

He stopped her. "Please, Kristi, your breasts are beautiful." His eyes swept over her, telling her just how beautiful, as one by one he fastened the buttons, starting at the bottom and working up. Leaving the top button open, he brushed a kiss into the hollow at the base of her throat, then raised his head to gaze into her eyes. "And I don't want you to feel embarrassed by what just happened between us either."

Kristi released the breath she'd been holding in a long sigh. "I won't," she whispered, feeling cherished.

Leaning over, he plucked one tiny white-gold flower and held it out to her. "Here, m'lady. A token of my thanks for the lovely memories you've given me today. I hope your memories will be good ones too," he said, wondering if she'd laugh at his corny speech.

Slowly Kristi sat up and stared at Dev, mesmerized by the way he was holding the delicate stem between his forefinger and thumb, as though afraid he'd crush it.

What a tender, tender man, she thought, accepting the flower from him. "Yes, Dev. They will be good memories."

Yes, they would be good memories, Kristi thought, as she rested her head against the side window of the plane and stared blindly at the tiny flower she held cupped in her hand. But did she want more memories of Dev to keep her warm in her old age? He was leaving in three nights, and she wouldn't see him again. Did she want a three-night affair?

Heaven help her, that might be just what she wanted, Kristi thought, wondering why she'd gone from wanting him to kiss her to wanting him to make love to her within a matter of a few heated moments. True, there was this sexual attraction between them that made her yearn for him, but there was also much more. She couldn't be falling in love with Dev, could she?

She blinked and the flower came into focus. She loved him . . . she loved him not . . . she loved him. . . .

The flower had five tiny golden petals.

She blinked and looked again. Now, who was being foolish!

Lifting her head from the cool window, she placed the flower in her tally book and carefully closed it. "Let's forget the grid and go home," she said, raising her voice over the noise of the engine.

Dev glanced at her in concern. "Are you all right?"

"I'm fine." She just needed time to sort out her feelings about Dev, and she couldn't do it sitting next to him in the confines of the small plane. His presence, his overwhelming masculinity made it impossible for her to think straight.

Dev turned the plane toward camp, then stole another longer look at Kristi. What was she thinking? She seemed so remote . . . like the top of Mount McKinley covered with clouds, and he couldn't blame her after he'd almost made love with her and then put her aside.

Lord help him, he still ached to touch her, to make love with her, but he couldn't. Not when he wanted her to work for him. And, dammit, he'd flatten the first man who dared suggest that Kristi had slept with him to curry favors.

"We've got visitors," Dev said as he flew in over camp.

Kristi turned her head for a better look at the floatplane, which was moored beside Dev's Lake Amphibian. "King Oil," she said, spotting the distinctive flag on the fuselage. "Must be out looking for you."

If she were a porcupine, she'd be firing quills, Dev thought, wishing King Oil would disappear down a hole. "Damn. How did they know where to find me?"

"Moccasin telegraph."

"Yeah. I forgot about that. Well, let's go see who it is," he said, relinquishing the controls to Kristi.

The tall, tanned, black-haired man who strolled

down to the shore to meet them with Rex at his heels was a complete surprise. Dressed in black from his Stetson to his boots, he had Texas oil stamped over every inch of his powerful frame.

"Duke. What are you doing here?"

"I might ask the same thing of you, little brother?"

The two men squared off facing each other, Duke topping Dev by a couple of inches. Dev held out his hand, and it was quickly gripped by his brother's.

"Good to see you, Dev, even though I had to come to the north pole to do it." Removing his Stetson, Duke turned his attention to Kristi, who was patting the dog as she kept a wary eye on the men. "Heard in Fairbanks you were camping with Miss Bjornson. I really came to see her."

Straightening to her full height, Kristi glared at him, remembering what she'd thought the first time she'd met David King: He was a handsome, arrogant man with a heart to match his steel-gray eyes. He was a hard man who expected results. No doubt he'd come to find out why Dev hadn't delivered them.

"Really, Mr. King. What about?"

"I saw your father the day before last."

"You saw Dad? Why? How is he?" She wanted to ask many more questions—such as what bribe he'd offered him—but resisted the urge.

Replacing his Stetson, Duke pulled it down over his eyes. "He managed to convince the doctors to turn him loose. I flew him out to the lodge."

"You flew him? And left him out there by himself?" she asked, concern putting a bite in her voice.

"Mary went with him," Duke hastened to reassure her. "And she told me to tell you not to worry, she'd make sure he followed the doctor's orders."

"Mary'll do that, all right," Kristi said, relief washing away her anger and concern. The warmhearted widow who owned the café in Cordova was just what her father needed, and she hoped he'd finally realized the fact.

Removing an envelope from the inside pocket of his sheepskin coat, Duke handed it to her. "Your father asked me to give this to you."

Heedless of manners, Kristi ripped open the envelope and scanned the contents of the brief note. "But it says here that you knew nothing about his accident until now," she said, staring at Duke in confusion.

"That's right. We only received a report about the oil spill, not the accident."

Dev gazed at Kristi in dismay as he rapidly put two and two together and came up with an answer he didn't like one little bit. "Oil spill? Accident? You mean King Oil was responsible for your father's accident, Kristi?"

She nodded, and Dev swung around to face his brother. "Dammit, Duke, that's criminal. I told you years ago that your safety standards were deplorable, especially in the North."

"I know you did, and we're taking immediate steps to improve the conditions."

"Immediate isn't soon enough. Kristi's father was hurt."

Duke's aristocratic features softened just a fraction as he looked at Kristi. "I know. That's why I'm here. To apologize and to see what we can do to help. I'm sorry it's taken me so long, Kristi, but I just discovered your letter. The Baron's been ill. It was in his mail."

"Father's ill? What's wrong?" Dev asked quietly.

"Dev, the Baron's had a stroke."

"Is . . . is he—?" Suddenly aware that Kristi had taken his hand, Dev gave her a grateful smile.

"He's fine, but madder than a yella jacket that he's been forced to take things easy."

"Why didn't anyone tell me?"

Duke's eyes rested on their clasped hands. "He forbade it. He didn't want you coming home because you felt sorry for him."

"The old fool."

"I'm looking at a young fool who's too idealistic for his own good."

"You mean you really aren't working for your father?" Kristi asked, her mind reeling with the implications of everything she'd just heard.

Dev shook his head. "No."

"You're not even on speaking terms with him? You honestly didn't know what happened this spring?"

"I read about the oil spill in the paper."

"And raised hell on the Hill," Duke added quietly.

"Oh, Dev," Kristi whispered in apology. "I thought you came up here to find a way to discredit me so I couldn't make my threat stick."

"What threat?" Dev asked, feeling as confused as Kristi looked.

Duke answered for her, his voice full of admiration. "To make life miserable for King Oil at every environmental hearing from now till doomsday. And she would've done just that, but we've decided to put all plans for drilling on the back burner until there are better safeguards for moving the oil down the coast. We have enough leases elsewhere to keep us busy for a few years. So you'll have to put your energies into fighting another cause, Kristi." The smile he gave her was tight and rusty as if he weren't sure he knew how to smile. "Why don't you give Dev a hand with his commission." Duke shifted his gaze to Dev. "She's highly qualified, and well respected, and an awesome opponent. I speak from experience."

Dev nodded his agreement. "You don't have to sell Kristi to me. I've been trying to convince her to join the commission ever since I arrived."

"So that's the reason you came north. The guys in Fairbanks couldn't imagine why you were here or what was keeping you so long." Duke glanced at their clasped hands again, then at Dev's face. "By the way, a TV crew was nosing around base camp asking questions about you, Dev. They'll probably show up someday soon."

Suddenly realizing she was still holding Dev's hand, Kristi released it and stepped back.

Dev felt a surprising sense of loss as she moved away. It had been so good to have her standing next to him, supporting him, giving him comfort.

"I came to put a marker on the King's grave," he said, correcting Duke's assumption.

Duke thumbed his Stetson up and stared at Dev in surprise. "Good Lord! Is it near here?"

"A few miles west of here."

Duke slammed his fist against his open hand, turned away, then swung around to face his brother again. "I'm ashamed of myself. In all the years I've been traveling back and forth, I've never taken the time to hunt up his grave. Neither, for that matter, have Dad or Dare, and they've both been through here countless times." Reaching out, he clasped Dev by the shoulders, giving him a long, thoughtful look. "Trust you, little brother, to do the right thing." His grip tightened. "But take one more step. Come home."

The poignancy of the moment was so great that Kristi couldn't bear to watch it. She moved down the beach, out of earshot, taking Rex with her.

"We'll see," Dev said, following Kristi with his gaze.

Duke released Dev and stepped back. "Don't leave it until too late because of your stubborn pride."

"We'll see."

"Madre misses you."

Dev smiled, thinking of his lovely mother. "And I miss her."

"And the ranch is going to pot without you."

"Nice try," Dev said, punching Duke lightly on the arm. "But that's Dare's baby, when he decides to settle down."

"The Duchess is growing weary of waiting for a great-grandchild," Duke said gruffly.

Dev laughed. "Need I remind you that she has three grandsons, and I'm the youngest. There's no reason why you can't remarry and produce an heir."

"Oh, yes there is, Dev. A very good reason." For one unguarded moment Duke's gray eyes were filled with longing, then the shutters came down again. "Well, little brother, you have a head start on the rest of us." Duke leaned forward and continued in a low voice. "Bring Kristi home. The Duchess is waiting."

"What are you talking about?"

"You love her, don't you?"

Dev stepped back and glared at his brother, surprised he would even suggest such a thing. "Lord, no."

"Well, you sure could've fooled me. There's a certain way a man looks at a woman when he—"

"Another word and you'll be mopping blood," he said, shaking his clenched fist under Duke's nose.

Duke's eyes narrowed as they measured the threatening fist, then searched his brother's face. "You mean, you haven't made love to that beautiful gal?"

Dev stared at his fist in amazement, then dropped it to his side. "That beautiful gal won't say yes to anything," he said ruefully, deciding it was time to lighten the mood. "She won't even let me put the marker on the grave until the little owl nesting on it learns how to fly."

Duke's harsh hoot of laughter brought Kristi back to the brothers. "What's so funny?"

"I was just telling Duke about the ookpik."

Lifting the cuff of his sleeve with a long forefinger, Duke glanced at the gold watch on his wrist. "I'd like to see the grave before I head south."

"I'll take you over, Duke. I sure could use some help lugging the marker up the hill." Dev gave Kristi a reassuring look. "But only to the brow. I'll wrestle it the rest of the way myself if the ookpik fledges before I have to leave."

"Be glad to give you a hand, but I'll take my plane and go on from there. I want to catch the evening flight."

"You can ride with me, Kristi," Dev offered, sliding his arm around her shoulders.

She gave him a quick hug, then stepped back. "You two should be alone for a while." Besides, she still needed to sort out her feelings for Dev—now more than ever.

"You mean you trust me?" he asked softly.

She gazed at him, eyes glowing as she whispered, "Yes."

Dev smiled at her, feeling as though he could move a mountain all by himself. Their relationship had just taken one gigantic step forward.

Restless with tension, Kristi couldn't just sit and think. She washed clothes, including Dev's. When she found herself standing with his jeans clutched against her breast, she finally admitted just how badly she felt about not trusting him.

But saints preserve her, she had more than enough reasons not to trust him. He'd flown in with a farfetched story only his mother would believe. But it had been true.

Why hadn't she believed him when she'd seen the grave?

Because she was afraid of the power King Oil had to destroy her. Time after time she'd seen people, big companies, even governments bow down to the oil barons. And she'd had the impudence to wave her tail feathers under the fox's nose.

As soon as she'd sent the letter she'd realized her threats were as hollow as a trumpeter's bones. Fear of the Baron's retaliation had caused her to misjudge his son and to continue to be suspicious despite all evidence to the contrary. There was no longer any reason to believe that Dev was one of the enemy. No need to mistrust him.

Did that mean she could love him?

Kristi snapped Dev's jeans twice and hung them on the line, refusing to think about the possibility. It was too soon to be falling in love with Dev. True, his kisses made her go all warm and buttery inside, and his eyes made her feel so very much a woman. But that wasn't love, was it?

And how did he feel about her? He'd almost made love to her that afternoon. Surely he must feel something for her . . . but it didn't have to be love. Hadn't he told her that he didn't want to fall in love with her?

Oh, Lord, this was confusing. Maybe she should insist that he leave. After all, she now knew he wasn't working for his father, and her reason for inviting him into camp was no longer valid. She'd even trust him enough to let him camp at King's Lake—if he wanted to.

What was taking Dev so long, anyway? He should've been back hours ago. Maybe he was having engine trouble. Maybe he'd crashed.

Take it easy, she admonished herself. He was a good pilot. But if he wasn't back by the time she'd hung up the wash, she was going after him, she promised herself as she hurriedly dumped the water.

The sight of Dev's plane on King's Lake settled the flutters in Kristi's stomach, but they returned when she spotted him lying on top of the hill. Had he broken a leg? Or worse?

She charged down the beach and up the hill. Cresting the brow, she caught sight of Dev and stopped dead, covering her mouth to stay her gasp of delight.

Dev was lying, propped up on his elbow, with the owlet perched on the upright toes of his left foot. The little bird was sound asleep. Slowly Dev turned his head to gaze at her, a funny expression on his face—partly awe, partly pain, and a whole lot of wonder.

On legs that threatened to collapse, Kristi crept forward. Sinking to the ground beside him, she wrapped her arms around her knees.

"How did you get into this mess?" she asked, her voice husky with the need to laugh.

The corner of Dev's mouth lifted in a wry smile. "When Duke left, I sat down to watch the owls. After a few minutes the little one crawled up there, and before I knew it he'd gone to sleep," Dev whispered.

Kristi's shoulders began to shake. "When did this happen?"

He rolled his eyes. "Hours ago. Do you think he's sick or something?"

Giving in to the ache inside her, Kristi laughed softly. "I think he recognized a good thing when he found it and isn't about to let go."

"You find this funny?"

"It's the dearest thing I've ever seen."

"Well, I sure hope he doesn't sleep much longer. My foot is about ready to drop."

"You could frighten him off."

"No way. Not after winning his trust."

Kristi sat, chin on bent knees, and watched Dev in silence, realizing he'd also meant those words for her. It was as though he knew her trust was still fragile and was telling her that he wouldn't do anything to frighten her. The dear tenderfoot, she thought, wondering when the name had become a term of endearment.

Probably when the angry swan had chased him down the beach, she realized, her lips curving in a smile at the memory. Lifting her head, she stared out at the lake. The swans had emerged from hiding and the cygnets were busily eating, while the cob guarded and the pen preened. She looked much better, and Kristi remembered the amazement she'd felt when the cob had tried to protect the pen. Tundra Swans were not known for their bravery, but this one had not deserted his mate when she needed his protection.

Just as Dev would also protect his mate with every last ounce of his strength, if the need arose.

Kristi felt her insides grow soft and warm as her gaze returned to Dev's foot. And who would've ever thought an owlet would crawl up on his foot and go to sleep? Snowies weren't as shy as the swans, but it usually took ages to gain their trust.

It had taken Dev a matter of minutes.

Even the mother was snoozing peacefully a short distance away, totally unconcerned about the plight of her chick.

Aware that Dev had been watching her, Kristi finally tilted her head and looked at him. The loving expression on his face stopped her heart. His eyes held hers, and for a few fluttering moments she could only sit and stare at him. When she couldn't bear to look at him any longer, she turned her head away, noting for the first time the marker which sat on the brow of the hill, well back of the grave. It was a five-feet high wooden statue of a Canada goose, wingtips curled in flight.

"That's the most beautiful carving I've ever seen," she said softly, wanting to get up and examine it but unwilling to frighten the owl.

"I asked a friend of mine to make it when I decided to come north. I wanted something symbolic," Dev said, thinking of the pendant in his breast pocket, which was becoming more and more symbolic with each fleeting hour.

She looked back at him to find him still watching her. "Why a Canada goose?"

"They winter in the wetlands on the ranch. Every fall grandfather would arrive home about the same time as the geese and he'd take me into the bayous to see them." He smiled at the memories. "I think that's when I first began to appreciate how important it is to protect the wildlife while we're busy exploiting this planet of ours."

She remembered something else he'd told her. "Is that why you've been involved in causes all your life?"

"It's a good part of the reason."

"I'm sorry I misjudged you," she said, knowing the apology was totally inadequate.

"After hearing what happened to your father, I can understand why you did." The look he gave her made her feel much better. "Duke was pretty upset about everything," he continued. "Especially your father."

"I didn't realize Duke was so human. He'd struck me as a coldhearted man." Except at the hearing, her conscience reminded her.

"He wasn't always that way."

"What happened?" Kristi asked, intrigued despite her reservations about the man.

"The usual. A woman broke his heart."

"So he doesn't believe in love?"

"Not for himself. But he believes in the love my parents have for each other and my grandmother's enduring love for my grandfather, despite the fact the King flew north with the honkers every spring."

Kristi looked at the marker again. "Your grandfather would be happy with the marker."

"I hope the Duchess will be too."

"If she has one shred of romance in her soul—and I suspect she has—she'll love it." Kristi remembered all the camera equipment they'd hauled up the hill the first day and was now stashed in the back of her plane. "And she'll love the pictures. You're a very special man to be doing this for her, Dev."

"It's something I've always wanted to do, but I just couldn't find the time until now." He gave her a slow, meaningful smile. "Thank goodness, because I wouldn't have met you."

Kristi glowed in the warmth of his smile, thinking how happy she was that Dev had come into her life. She didn't know how it was going to end, but she wouldn't have missed the experience of knowing him for anything in the world.

"Looks like Intrepid has decided to wake up," Dev said, bringing her out of her reverie.

Blinking away her thoughts, she focused on Dev's foot. The owlet was staring at them with one sleepy yellow eye. "Intrepid?"

"Suits him, don't you think?"

The name also suited Dev, Kristi thought, a soft smile playing about her lips.

Slowly the owl opened his other eye and gazed dreamily at them for a few minutes. Finally he pumped his wings a couple of times, then fell off Dev's foot to the ground. Unperturbed, he hopped up and down, flapping his wings.

Intrigued, Dev pulled his legs out of the way and leaned forward, urging the little owl into the air with quick bobs of his head. The ookpik hopped and flapped, then stopped.

Placing his hands on his chest, Dev flapped his elbows in encouragement. The ookpik flapped again. Dev followed suit.

And Kristi fell in love.

Nine

Kristi gripped her knees for dear life as the tundra turned, threatening to tumble her off the top of the world. She couldn't be in love with Dev, she thought in mounting panic. She didn't *want* to be in love with Devlin King. He was entirely wrong for her. He was a congressman from Texas, for heaven's sake. He lived about as far from Alaska as he could and still be in the Lower 48.

Dev flapped his elbows again.

It was too late, her heart told her. She loved him. She loved the dear tenderfoot.

With one last flap, Intrepid gave up his attempt and scurried off in search of his mother, who'd been watching from her perch on the grave.

Chuckling with delight, Dev turned toward Kristi. His wide smile faded into a self-conscious grin as he saw the expression on her face.

"I guess I looked pretty silly there. I kinda got carried away."

"You'd never look silly, no matter how hard you tried."

It was too soon to admit her love, Kristi thought, still struggling to come to terms with it herself. But she wanted to do something special so this moment would also be memorable for Dev.

Slowly she released her knees and reached out to take his hand. "Dev, would you do something for me?"

"Anything," he said, his eyes becoming misty green as he watched her.

Bedroom eyes, Kristi thought, wondering if she'd ever see how they'd look while they made love. She laughed breathlessly. "Wait until you hear what it is before you make that promise."

"I can't imagine you asking me to do anything I'd object to," he said, bringing her hand to his lips and brushing a kiss across her knuckles. There were many things he wanted to do for Kristi, to Kristi, with Kristi, and he hoped she wouldn't object to any of them—but he shouldn't even be thinking about them, he warned himself.

"Would you settle your differences with your father as soon as you get home?"

His eyes widened in surprise as he allowed her to draw his hand into her lap. Trust Kristi to cut straight to the heart of the matter. None of the women he dated had even known he was at odds with his father and separated from his loved ones, but then he'd never allowed anyone to get close enough to find out. Until Kristi had flown into his life. Kristi, who was once again putting his welfare above her own personal feelings.

"Kristi, why would you ask me to do that?" he asked huskily. "You don't even like my father."

"It's obvious your family is important to you. Every time you talk about them your voice is full of love." She turned his hand over, studying the palm, looking for inspiration. "How long have you been estranged from them?"

He closed his hand around hers and absently stroked her wrist with his thumb. "Three years."

She glanced up at him, her eyes bright with concern. "Oh, Dev, that's too long to hold a grudge. What did you and the Baron fight about?"

His thoughts were so full of Kristi that it took Dev a moment to remember. "I wanted to run for congress, and the Baron wanted me to stay home and help run the company. King Oil is his life, and he couldn't understand why I had to do my own thing. He told me that if I left, I should stay away for good." He shook his head, smiling ironically. "I kept hoping he'd change his mind after I won the election, but he didn't."

"Ah, but he admired you for your stand, Dev," she said with conviction, barely resisting the urge to kiss him. But every time she kissed Dev, her good intentions went up in smoke, and right now she had to keep her wits about her.

"What do you mean?" Dev asked, leaning closer to the woman who in four short days had become so very special to him.

His breath warmed her cheek, fanning an even greater longing to melt into his arms. She battled the feelings, knowing there was more at stake than her own needs.

"Your father could've prevented you from winning the election with a few words in the right places."

He frowned, lost in thought for a moment, then nodded. "You're right. I kept expecting him to oppose me, but he didn't. Not even when I was up for reelection. I always wondered why."

"I imagine it was his way of saying he was sorry. Go see him, Dev," she urged.

Dev could only sit and smile at her as her concern washed over him, making him feel very special, very cared for, very much loved. "I will, as soon as I get home," he finally said. Lifting her hand again, he brushed a kiss along the inside of her wrist. "Thank you, sweetheart." Another kiss. "How did you get to be so wise?"

The kisses flowed like warm honey along her arm

to her heart. It pooled there, spinning into cotton candy and making her feel as though she were going to burst. She had to do something to break the spiral, or she'd be swept away by these new emotions. She wasn't ready for them. Yet.

"Watching owls," she said breathlessly, and was relieved when Dev threw back his head and laughed.

Relieved but also disappointed, she admitted as he pulled her to her feet and they walked hand in hand down the hill.

She'd wanted Dev to kiss her.

Thankful the cold ritual of his nightly bath was over, Dev headed for his tent. Rounding the pingo, he took one look at Kristi's tent, and dropped the plastic bucket on his toe. With a muffled curse he leaned over and retrieved the bucket, then slowly straightened.

Kristi hadn't finished her bath.

Backlit by the sun reflecting off the lake, the tent walls revealed only a shadow, but it was enough. More than enough. He could see her towel moving across the curve of her breasts, and he gripped his towel tighter as his memory filled in the flesh and blood details—the warmth of her ivory skin, the rosy tips of her nipples. Her towel dipped lower down the hollow plane of her belly, and he groaned, wanting nothing more than to be in the tent with Kristi, drying her body, touching her all over. Making love with her.

But he couldn't make love with her. The reasons he had given her that morning—was it only that morning?—were still valid. He didn't want even a breath of scandal to touch Kristi. Maybe it was already too late, he thought wryly. If Duke's comments were any indication of things to come, he'd be bashing noses as soon as he and Kristi reached Washington. Because he was not going to leave

Alaska without Kristi. She was going to come south with him—where she would be safe.

The thought had begun simmering in his mind at the gravesite and now burst forth in a full-blown realization. He wanted, above all else, to keep Kristi safe.

Kristi began donning clothes, and Dev moved closer, torn between the soul-deep desire to enter the tent and the knowledge that if he did, he would be damning his soul. For keeping Kristi safe also meant keeping her safe from himself.

The war was still waging when Kristi, basin in hand and clad in a navy Eskimo parka shell and long johns, emerged from the tent and straightened to find him watching her. After giving a little shiver she walked away from him, carrying her basin of water toward the slop hole.

He started after her, then stopped. What the hell had gotten into him anyway? One moment he wanted her for himself. One moment he was nobly telling himself that he shouldn't make love to her, only to get upset because she was ignoring him.

Kristi had gotten to him, he acknowledged, the thought sinking like lead to the pit of his stomach. Beautiful Kristi who had turned his world upside down with her caring ways. Tempting Kristi, who could keep him in constant turmoil with just one glance from her glimmering eyes. He couldn't think straight when he was around her, much less keep his emotions under control.

Whipping the towel off his shoulders, he hung it up on the makeshift clothesline beside his jeans, then carried his bucket to the kitchen. When Kristi joined him, he was sitting on the ground, his hand tucked inside his bomber jacket, holding the box which contained the ivory pendant. She sidled past without looking at him and laid her basin on the table.

The ivory was cold, he knew, and he could imagine how it longed for the warmth of her skin. Slowly he removed his hand from temptation and looked at the sky.

"I wish it was dark enough to see the Milky Way," he said thoughtfully, then sat up abruptly as Rex licked his face. "Beat it, mutt," he said, then relented and began rubbing Rex's belly when the dog flopped down beside him.

Kristi laughed in delight as the interaction between man and dog brought things back to normal, erasing the tension she'd been feeling all evening. "Why the Milky Way?"

"As a kid I was fascinated by the stars." His hand slowed, then stopped. "I was always disappointed that I couldn't see the Northern Cross."

"The Cygnus."

"Yes, the swan." He leaned forward and gave Kristi a meaningful look. "She's flying south, you know."

Kristi sank onto the campstool. "I know," she admitted reluctantly. She realized where the conversation was leading; they'd had it at least once a day during the last four days.

"I wish you'd come south with me, Kristi. You'd be perfect for the commission."

"I can't, Dev. I have to finish this project," she said, knowing it was a poor excuse. But she wasn't ready to go with him just because she had fallen in love with him. In fact, her love for him made it all the more important that she refuse. For hadn't he said that he didn't want to fall in love with her, didn't want a crusader for a wife, didn't even want to make love with her for fear he'd harm her reputation?

"I could hold the position open until you're ready to take it. You'd be finished here by October, wouldn't you?"

"Yes."

"And you could write your report and finish your thesis in Washington."

"Yes."

He frowned, momentarily distracted as Rex sat up

and growled. Reaching out, he patted Rex's head, but the dog rose and trotted away from camp. "Then what's stopping you from coming?" he asked, turning his attention back to Kristi.

"I have other obligations."

"What obligations? You no longer have any reason to fight King Oil."

Kristi stared at him in consternation as she realized he was right. She didn't have to oppose King Oil at environmental hearings; they weren't expanding. And her father didn't need her anymore; he had Mary and the lodge. So what was she going to do with her life?

"I really do want you to come work for me, Kristi," Dev said, his eyes compelling her to agree. "The commission is one of the most important things I've ever undertaken, and I don't want it to fail. I need you, Kristi."

If the commission was the most important thing he'd ever undertaken, then he definitely didn't need her, Kristi thought. She'd fail him just as she'd failed the last people who had counted on her. Unable to look at him any longer, she jumped to her feet and moved the campstool in under cover, then checked the lids on the two wooden crates.

He watched her in silence, but rose to follow her as she left the tent. "Kristi?"

"I'd screw things up," she muttered, her nerve endings screaming with tension again.

"What are you talking about?"

"I told you before that I've only made one presentation in my life, and it was an absolute fiasco."

"I find that hard to believe."

"Believe it," she said, reaching down to pat Rex, who'd returned to her side, the hair on the back of his neck bristling. "What's the matter, Rex? Did the wolverine come back?"

Dev stared into the gloom but saw nothing except empty tundra. Out on the lake, a loon called hauntingly to its mate. The sound touched the loneliness in his soul.

"I don't see anything," he said, moving to stand beside Kristi.

She wished he weren't standing so close. "Me neither. Guess he must have chased it away."

Dev lay his arm against her back, resting his hand on her shoulder. She made an effort to relax as he began kneading the muscles at the base of her neck.

"What happened at the hearing, Kristi?"

Damn. She'd hoped the diversion with Rex had sidetracked Dev, but she should've known he wouldn't give up so easily. "Ask Duke, he was there."

"He said you were great."

"Your brother must've had a convenient memory lapse. I made a complete fool of myself. I took one look at all the people in the audience, and everything I wanted to say went out of my head. Then everything started closing in on me, the people, even the walls of the room. I'd still be standing there if Duke hadn't rescued me by asking the company's lawyer to repeat the question. Consequently, I blew the opportunity to stop the project." She glanced up at him again, her lips firm with conviction. "So you see, Dev, I'd be an albatross around your neck. Get someone else to head up your task force."

He considered her thoughtfully. "I can understand why you don't like speaking in public, Kristi, but don't you think it's time you overcame your fears?"

She tried to draw away, but he wouldn't let her go.

"You have no right to criticize me," she said, objecting to the feeling of being pushed, of being trapped. "You're just like my father. You both have the ability to charm a partridge out of a tree, to hold an audience in the palm of your hand, to make the very mundane sound interesting. You have no idea what it's like to be stumped for words, to feel like a blathering idiot. And you're both pushing me to do something I can't do."

"You're selling yourself short, Kristi," he said, gentling his hold. "I've spent the last four nights listening to you talk, and I haven't been bored for one single moment. When you get going on a subject close to your heart, you'd make an owl wake up and take notice."

His grin flashed, and she laughed softly, thinking—as she was certain he was—of little Intrepid. "But you're just one person." She sobered abruptly. "Put me in front of a crowd and I freeze."

"You could make-believe you were talking only to me," he said, nestling his free hand against her throat.

"You and how many hundred others?" Her voice broke as his thumb touched the corner of her mouth. If Dev was in the audience, she'd never remember what to say, she'd be too busy thinking about him, loving him . . . and that was the main reason why she shouldn't take the job, she reminded herself sternly. "Anyway, all this talk is academic. I don't want your job."

Beginning to feel more than a little desperate, Dev took a deep breath and tried again. "You're selling yourself short, Kristi. I'm offering you a job anyone in your business would pluck pinfeathers to land. A job that will open doors that could lead to a lifetime of opportunities. And you're afraid to take it."

"I am not afraid."

"Oh, yes you are, Kristi. And until you face your fears you won't be happy, won't feel complete."

He had hit the nail on the head, and she wished he couldn't read her so well. His ability to see right into her soul frightened her, made her feel vulnerable. "Please, Dev, just leave me alone. I can't take the job."

Slowly his thumb traced the outline of her mouth, then brushed back and forth against the fullness of her bottom lip. The sensation almost drove her crazy.

His curled forefinger tilted her chin up. "Should I use my so-called charm to persuade you?" he whispered a heartbeat before his lips captured hers.

The kiss exploded through her like a skyrocket, fueled by the desire that had been sparking in her all day. It set her body sizzling with need, and she knew that it would take very little effort for him to charm her into submission.

All he had to do was keep kissing her.

Eagerly she granted his tongue entry. Suddenly her knees buckled, and she swayed toward him, her arms going around his waist for support. With one hand, he braced her neck and head, while the other clasped her bottom and nudged her against his straining manhood in time with his probing tongue. Wave after wave of desire swept through her until she was trembling.

She arched against him, wanting him. She'd wanted him before, but the wanting was a hundred times more intense now that she knew she loved him. And her love made her extremely vulnerable to Dev's charm.

Dev's charm. In another moment she'd succumb, she knew. Making a supreme effort, she slipped out from under his arm and stared up at him, her lips quivering.

"What's the matter, Kristi?" he asked, his eyes hazy with desire and bewilderment.

She rubbed the back of her neck. "I don't like the way you were holding me."

He lifted a trembling hand toward her, then shoved it through his unruly hair. "Holding you?"

"By the neck. And just what are you trying to charm me to do?" she asked, folding her arms protectively across her breasts. "Work for you? Go to bed with you? Or both? And what would your colleagues have to say about that?"

Dev stared at her in dismay as her words and the hurt in her eyes struck him to the core. Hadn't he just vowed he wouldn't make love to her for that very same reason? What the hell was the matter with him, anyway? He wouldn't blame Kristi if she set him adrift on an ice floe.

After giving him another soulful look, which stabbed him in his heart, she called sharply to Rex and stumbled toward her tent.

Pulling himself together, Dev strode after her, wary of the dog who kept looking over his shoulder as he reluctantly followed his mistress into the tent. "Wait, Kristi. At least let me apologize."

She snapped the flap shut in his face, clutching it with shaking hands as she waited for his next move. If he tried to force his way in, she wouldn't fight him . . . and despite his growls, Rex wouldn't be any protection. The dog *liked* Dev, for heaven's sake.

Only Dev's soft voice entered the tent. "I didn't mean to come on so strong, Kristi, or to hold you so tightly. And as for charming you, you've got it all wrong. You're the one who's charmed me. Completely. From the moment we met."

Slowly Kristi raised the flap and looked up into Dev's handsome face. His eyes shone with sincerity. She drew a deep breath into her aching lungs, then let it out as her mind continued to stew. "I'm sorry, Dev. I don't know what got into me. I'm so confused right now that I hardly know which end is up."

"You're not the only one." Bracing one hand on the tent frame, he leaned over and brushed a kiss across her lips. "The only thing I know for certain is that I want to keep you safe," he said huskily.

Before she could respond, he pushed himself away and strode toward his tent, leaving Kristi more confused then ever.

Ten

Dev lay listening to his jeans flapping in the wind, wishing he'd at least thanked Kristi for washing his clothes. One more thing she'd done for him. Would it ever end?

Yes, it was going to end, he thought, tomorrow, when she told him to leave. And this time he'd have no excuse to stay. He knew he could place the marker on the gravesite without disturbing the owls. They trusted him. If only Kristi trusted as much.

True, she'd trusted him enough to let him go to the gravesite with Duke, however his recent actions had destroyed that trust. He had sensed she didn't like the way he'd been holding her, but he'd continued to hold her, and the knowledge that he'd resorted to such desperate tactics made him cringe. No wonder Kristi had objected.

He heard Rex whine and the sound of the zipper as Kristi opened the tent flap. "What's the matter, boy?" she said, her voice sounding sleepy.

She must be dead tired, Dev thought, as he threw off the covers and shoved his feet into his moccasins. The least he could do was make sure Rex was safe.

Opening the flap, he caught sight of Kristi, standing in the twilight looking sexy in her long johns. Desire gripped his loins bringing him up short. He'd already made one mistake. If he went out there, he might do something he'd be ashamed of for the rest of his life.

He half turned, then stopped as Rex bounded toward the pingo barking furiously. Remembering their unwanted visitor, Dev grabbed the harpoon which lay on the floor beside the door and scrambled outside.

"Stay back, I'll get my gun," Kristi yelled as she ran past him toward her tent.

Ignoring her order, Dev took off toward the sound of Rex's barking. He charged around the pingo, then halted abruptly as the meanest animal he'd ever seen turned from Rex to snarl at him. It was a wolverine, and it had Rex cornered. There was no time to wait for Kristi and the gun. Against those wicked claws, massive teeth, and powerful jaws, Rex didn't have a chance.

Dev lunged, thrusting the harpoon at the wolverine. It leapt, fangs bared, straight for him. Instinctively, Dev swept the harpoon upward, driving it into the wolverine. Delayed reaction took over, and Dev's legs began trembling as Rex bounded forward, barking and growling, to stand guard over the intruder.

Just then Kristi raced around the pingo, the shotgun poised for action. She paused momentarily, taking in Rex, the dead animal, and the half-dressed hero, then dropped her gun and ran toward Dev, her arms wide.

"Oh, Dev, Dev. You could've been killed," she cried, throwing her arms around him and hugging him to her.

Dev held her in triumph, knowing how the cob felt when he was welcomed by his mate. "I'm fine, Kristi. It didn't even touch me," Dev said, trying to reassure her.

His words and the feel of his solid body weren't

enough. Stepping back slightly, Kristi ran her palms over his chest, her eyes straining in the dim light, searching every inch of skin. "Are you sure it didn't bite you or scratch you?"

Dev laughed softly. "I'm sure, Kristi."

"Why would you do such a brave, foolish thing?"

The warmth of her eyes sent a wave of dizziness through him, and he wondered if she could feel his heart pounding beneath her hand.

"I couldn't let anything happen to Rex," he said huskily.

Reaching up, she brushed a kiss across his lips. "Thank you for saving Rex's life." With a shudder she leaned her head against his shoulder. "But if anything had happened to you . . ."

Dev gazed down at her, knowing with a certainty that would last a lifetime that Kristi had become the most precious person in the world to him. But with the certainty came a bone-gripping fear, and he wrapped his arms around her and held her close. "What if the wolverine had attacked you and you didn't have a gun?"

She raised her head and smiled at him. "There you go, worrying again."

"If anything happened to you, I think I would die. I—" With a groan, he claimed her lips while the unspoken words whispered into his heart. *I love you. I love you. I love you.*

His heart expanded, and he continued to kiss her, to pour his love into her. Suddenly everything made sense—the way he'd felt when he'd first seen her, his need to protect her, the turmoil in his mind every time he thought about leaving her there alone.

When finally his whole body felt as if it would burst, he raised his head and gazed into her starry eyes. She murmured a protest and reached up for him again, but he held back, shaking his head. "Kristi, Kristi, I want to make love with you."

"And I want to make love with you, Dev," she said

breathlessly, everything inside her wanting to be his, to make him hers, to be one with this man.

He swept her into his arms and effortlessly carried her into her tent. Lowering her onto the bedroll, he knelt before her, his hands on her shoulders.

"Dev, there's something you should probably know," she said, her lashes covering her eyes briefly before she raised them again. "I've never made love before."

His face reflected his surprise and pleasure. "But I thought . . . not with Fergus? Oh, Kristi, sweetheart." He hugged her to him, then let her go, making himself relax. "Then we'll take things slow and easy, and chart the stars together."

Slowly he covered her lips, then all thoughts of slow and easy disappeared as the need which had simmered between them all day boiled over. With a moan that sounded like a plea, Kristi demanded more. Dev gave it, filling her mouth with his tongue, savoring her sweetness, seeking. And she gave in equal measure, sipping the masculine taste of him until he, too, was moaning. The moans turned to murmurs, then to breathless gasps as they gave and took and gave some more.

Gradually Kristi became aware that she was clasping Dev so tightly, she could barely breathe. She eased her hold, but began running her hands feverishly up and down his back, needing to touch him, to reassure herself that he was unharmed. Her stomach was still knotted with worry—worry that had begun when Dev hadn't returned from King's Lake and then resurfaced when he'd almost been attacked by the wolverine. Her body still ached from wanting him, the ache even greater now that she'd almost lost him. And her heart still sung with the discovery that she loved him.

Dev braced himself on one arm and raised his body off hers. His free hand found the curve of her breast, but it was covered by a barrier of cotton and he wanted to touch Kristi. With trembling fingers he released a button then slipped his hand inside and covered her breast. It filled his palm perfectly, as though it belonged there. She was satiny smooth and downy soft, but it wasn't enough to just touch her.

"I need to see you again, Kristi," he said huskily, as he began unbuttoning the top button. "I never thought long johns were sexy. But on you, they're sexier than sin."

"I'm glad you like them," she said, her voice a gentle purr.

"Sexy or not, they're in the way." His eyelids grew heavy with desire as he raised her up and slipped her long johns off her shoulders and down her arms. The light was much dimmer in the tent, but she still glowed, white-gold and ivory against the darkness. "You're so lovely," he said as he eased her back on the mattress and bent over her. He inhaled deeply, loving the sweet fragrance of roses that clung to her skin. "I want to taste you."

She moaned as his lips tugged her pouting nipple, sending ripple after ripple of sensations through her. It was as if once the sensations had begun, they wouldn't stop, traveling in wider and wider circles until they touched every part of her body . . . bringing her alive and totally aware of her desire.

Suddenly she wanted more, she wanted him in her. She murmured her need as her fingers found their way under the waistband of his jogging suit.

Dev went completely motionless as she explored further, then released him from the confines of his clothes. Growing bolder, she caressed him more intimately. And with each caress the fullness, the pressure, the aching need to be deep inside Kristi grew and grew.

Raising his head, he gazed down at her, his eyes dark with desire. "Oh, sweetheart, I love what you do to me," he said, his breath coming in quick gasps.

She gazed back with stars shimmering in her eyes. "And I want you next to me, in me," she whispered urgently. He felt so strong, so alive, so virile.

Laughing huskily, he began removing their clothes, a difficult feat because her hands restricted his movement. But he wouldn't have it any other way.

"Is this better?" he finally asked as he nestled into the cradle of her thighs.

"Much better than this morning," she said, reveling in the weight of his body against hers, his throbbing hardness against her pulsing softness.

Was it only this morning? Dev wondered. It seemed like ages since he'd halted their lovemaking. But soon they would be one . . . and he'd never have to be alone again.

Was it only this morning? Kristi wondered. She'd traveled such a long journey in awareness since then, almost as far as the swans traveled when they migrated south. She was in a new land when it came to her feelings about Dev—and the land was a bit scary. But with Dev as her guide, she soon would discover the heights of love.

Bracing himself on one arm, he bent to take her lips in a long kiss while his fingers found her, entered her, prepared her. She whimpered, reaching for him, caressing his heat and hardness as a quivering feeling filled her body. She was ready for Dev, she knew, ready to go with him to a place she'd never been before.

"Dev. Please. I want to see your face."

He raised his head, gazing down at her with reassuring love as she made room for him between her thighs. She watched his eyes go bright with desire as he found her waiting warmth, then grow dark with concern as he felt her last barrier of resistance. Slowly but steadily he eased his way through, his eyes growing wide with wonder as she surrounded him, accepted him, pulled him deeper.

"Oh, Dev. That feels so good," she said, crooning with pleasure. "You fill me completely."

"It's heaven." Carefully he pressed on until he was nestled deeply in her silk-lined nest.

"You touched my soul."

Her words had touched his soul, and he trembled with the desire to make her completely his. Instead he waited, allowing her to adjust to him before he began to move. She followed the call, arching to meet him, then surging ahead to chart new horizons, joyfully seeking the final discovery.

And suddenly she arrived in the land full of shooting stars and northern lights and wondrous sensations. And Dev was right behind her.

"Ah, Kristi, Kristi, Kristi," he whispered before collapsing into her arms. "We're home, sweetheart. Safe and sound."

Kristi hugged him close. This was where she wanted to be. Holding her man. Loving her man. Keeping him safe now that the danger had passed. She was home. And she never wanted to leave.

Dev rested against her for long moments, then rolled onto his back and lifted her on top. Finding the corner of the sleeping bag, Kristi pulled it up over her and snuggled against Dev. They lay in contented silence, Kristi probing the heavy muscles in Dev's shoulder with her fingertips, and Dev running his hand lightly up and down her back.

She was perfect for him, Dev thought, absolutely perfect.

"You've just made me the happiest man in the world," he whispered against her hair, afraid that if he spoke louder he'd be shouting for joy. "But more than that you've filled the void in my life—in my soul."

Filled to the brim with love herself, Kristi lay in Dev's arms, silently nuzzling his salty neck. For the first time in her life she wished she had the gift of gab so she could find words to match his. But surely he knew she loved him. Hadn't she just shown him how much?

She started to say something but the words were smothered under a yawn. After another huge yawn she snuggled against Dev's warm, solid body, gave a sigh of contentment, and immediately went to sleep.

Dev hugged her close, wishing he could hold her for the rest of his life. Kristi was everything he'd ever dreamed of, everything he'd ever wanted in a woman, in a wife.

Wife. Suddenly everything became very clear, very focused, and Dev knew why he'd been in such a turmoil these last few days. He didn't want Kristi to work for him, he wanted her to marry him.

True, she was a crusader. However, he wouldn't have it any other way, for he, too, was a crusader, and he wouldn't be happy if he were married to a woman who wasn't involved in a cause. That was the reason, he suspected, that none of the society women he'd dated had held his interest past the first date.

Life with Kristi would be exciting. Even if she couldn't work for the commission, she wouldn't have to give up her birds. He could just see himself, pacing the floor of their Georgetown apartment, worrying because she hadn't come home from a field trip to the Chesapeake. And she'd breeze in, sun kissed and windblown in her mud boots, just in time to entertain their guests. Which she'd do royally, with a natural ease that would make everyone feel very much at home.

He could also picture her with their fair-headed son on her knee, telling him stories of how she'd met his father. Later there'd be grandchildren to hear the story and, if the good Lord were willing, great-grandchildren.

But first things first. Kristi hadn't even told him that she loved him.

Maybe he should wake Kristi up and tell her he

loved her, Dev thought, then discarded the idea. He wanted to know for certain that Kristi loved him before he said the words aloud. True, she had made love with him, but she could have been swept away by other emotions—concern for him and gratitude because he'd saved Rex's life. He didn't want either. He wanted Kristi's love.

Kristi woke to find herself alone, and she felt cheated. She'd wanted to wake up in the arms of her lover and slowly discover the length and breath of his beautiful body—the one pleasure she'd been denied during their lovemaking. She'd been too over-whelmed by the need to reassure herself that Dev was alive to take the time to really look at him. Now they had the time. But where was Dev?

Why had he left her bed? Didn't he want to make love with her again? Maybe she should tell him she loved him. No, she couldn't do that, not after he had warned her that he didn't want to fall in love with her. But what would he want from her now?

And what did she want from him?

The questions kept flashing through her mind as she slowly sat up and began dressing. Each question only brought more questions, and finally she gave up her quest for answers. Maybe none of this would matter; Dev might be packed up, ready to leave. Forcing a bright smile to her lips, she ventured outside to meet her fate.

Dev glanced up from the camp stove, then strolled toward her, a mug of coffee in each hand and Rex at his heels. "You look beautiful this morning, Kristi," he said, bending down to brush a gentle, all too brief kiss against her lips before handing her a mug.

With trembling hands, she took the mug and gazed at him shyly over the rim. He wasn't sleepy eyed as he normally was in the morning. In fact his eyes were misty green with memories. "Thank you," she whispered, her throat tight with her own memories, of how beautiful she'd felt in his arms, how totally alive.

"Any regrets?"

"No, Dev. Making love with you was the most wonderful thing that has ever happened to me. But . . ."

"But?"

"What's going to happen now?"

"I don't know." He waited, hoping she'd say she loved him or at least offer to come south and work for him.

"I don't know either." She waited, torn between hope and fear that he would tell her that he loved her. She had grown up with the belief that love meant commitment and commitment meant marriage, but did she really want to marry Dev?

And did Dev want to marry her? All he'd done so far was ask her to work for him. If she took the job, she'd wind up sleeping with him . . . become one of his Washington women. On the other hand, if he asked her to marry him, she knew beyond a shadow of a doubt that he wouldn't want her to come north with the birds. And she wasn't willing to give them up. She loved Alaska, loved working with her birds. She also loved Dev.

Would he make her choose between them?

The silence became more charged with each passing moment until Kristi couldn't bear the uncertainty any longer. "You don't have to hang around, Dev. I'm sure you could put up the marker without disturbing the owls."

"Do you want me to leave?" he asked, his heart diving to the soles of his feet.

"No," she said, ignoring the voice telling her to send him away while she still had the willpower. But she couldn't; she'd let him make the choice. "You have responsibilities in Washington. You must be anxious to get back."

His heart lifted. "The commission can do without me for a few more days, but I'll have to leave on Sunday at the latest. I know Intrepid might not fly before then, but I'd like to hang around in case he does. If it's all right with you?"

"Yes," she whispered.

"Thank you." He took a deep breath. "And ah, Kristi, I just want you to know I won't pressure you to make love again. Don't get me wrong, there's nothing I'd rather do. But just because we made love last night doesn't give me the right to assume you'll be willing tonight." He turned away abruptly, raking his hand through his hair. "Ah, hell. I'm making a mess of this."

Kristi stared at his back, feeling disappointment and relief. Her body, heart, and soul yearned to make love with Dev, however, she was also afraid that if they did make love again, her body, heart, and soul would be torn to shreds when he left.

"Then we'll carry on, Dev, like we were before," she said, pushing away the knowledge that things could never be the same between them.

The next two days were pure heaven and pure hell. Kristi sat beside Dev in the plane, breathing deeply of his unique scent and basking in the warmth of his smile. For the most part he flew one-handed with the other resting lightly on her neck or knee. He didn't caress her or make any suggestive moves. His hand was just there. And she loved it.

As she loved the way he opened up and talked to her in the evenings. Listening to the stories about his family, Kristi realized how much he loved them and missed them. To her private chagrin, she admitted she'd probably like his family if she ever had the chance to meet all of them.

She laughed often as he regaled her with tales of life in Washington and was surprised to find herself thinking she'd enjoy meeting his friends too. They sounded like such interesting people.

But his stories of his crusades, his triumphs, and his failures gave her pause to think.

"You expect too much of yourself, Dev," she said in concern. "You can't take on the whole world."

"I know. But I can't *not* get involved. I don't understand how people can stand around and do nothing when they see something that needs to be done."

"You also expect too much of others."

"Maybe I do, but I believe that people are essentially good, that they want to be the best they can be."

"And you're constantly being disappointed." Kristi knew deep in her heart that Dev was disappointed in her unwillingness to work for him, and in the reason behind her refusal. He was right. It was time she did something about overcoming her fear of speaking to a large audience. And until she did, she wouldn't be the best *she* could be.

However it no longer mattered. Dev hadn't said a word about her working for him since they had made love, and Kristi knew that he couldn't, in good conscience, offer her the job.

Dev's crooked smile pulled her attention back to him. "Sometimes I get discouraged, but I love what I'm doing. I can't think of anything I'd rather do."

"You're a crusader, if I've ever seen one," Kristi said, giving him a quick hug. "And I'm glad you are. The country needs men like you."

Dev wrapped his arms around Kristi and hugged her back. She would be good for him, he knew. She'd reel him in when he went off on a tangent and give him a hand up when he was feeling down. Lord, how he loved her.

Oh how she loved Dev, Kristi thought. Everything she learned about him made her love him more. How was she going to survive when he left?

Dev wondered how he was ever going to survive without Kristi. If he were smart, he'd be making love to her at this very moment, forging a bond between them—like the bond that existed between the female swan and her mate—making Kristi so physically dependent on him, she'd follow him to the ends of the earth. But physical dependence wasn't enough. He wanted her to love him with her heart and her soul. But he had to work fast.

By midafternoon of the second day, time ran out.

Eleven

Carrying the lunch bag and blanket, Dev slowly followed Kristi over the crest of the hill, dreading what he would find. "Are they gone?" he whispered.

"No, there they are." Kristi pointed to the powder puff of feathers sitting in a shallow depression next to the grave. Nearby the mother stood guard.

Dev laughed, feeling lighthearted with relief. "And Intrepid's sound asleep again. He sure isn't taking this flying business very seriously, is he?"

"He'll fly when he's ready."

"Let's sneak closer so we can watch him."

"Do you think it's safe?" Kristi asked, her blue eyes sparkling with laughter. "Remember what happened the last time you got too close?"

The creases in Dev's cheeks deepened as he smiled. "I'm willing to take the chance if you are."

The way she felt about Dev, she'd take a chance on anything he wanted to do. "Lead on, *Cheechako*," she said with a sweep of her hand.

Carefully selecting a patch of thick moss sheltered from the wind and warmed by the sun, he spread the blanket on top of it. With a gallant bow, he extended his hand. She accepted it, sinking gracefully to the ground. He stretched out beside her and smiled into her eyes for what seemed like an eternity.

Finally he roused himself enough to shed his bomber jacket. "It's hot today."

"Most likely it's the last warm day of summer," Kristi said, admiring the way his brown sweater emphasized the width of his shoulders and the strength of his arms. The temptation to slide her hands underneath it and caress his hard muscular flesh was almost too much to resist. When a sigh escaped her lips, he turned to look at her with soft, sexy eyes. She drew in a deep breath as a hot flash of desire burned through her.

Dev watched her breasts rise then fall and wondered if she'd deliberately worn that snug blue shirt to drive him crazy. It molded her breasts to perfection, and the memory of what lay underneath made him ache.

With a trembling hand, she passed him a bannock and ham sandwich. With a hand that also trembled, he took it. Their hands touched, lingered, then reluctantly fell away.

Laughing softly, they both lowered their gazes, then glanced up to catch each other looking. They laughed again, more breathlessly this time.

Dev's throat was so tight, he couldn't speak, let alone swallow. He crumbled his sandwich with restless fingers as he continued to look at her.

As Kristi watched Dev, her mouthful of bannock turned to chalk, and it was all she could do to choke it down. Rummaging in the lunch bag, she found the apples and handed one to Dev.

Kristi was achingly aware of the need Dev could create with just the touch of his eyes. Would he leave without making love with her again?

Dev longed to make love with Kristi once more in this land men called barren. It wasn't barren. It was alive with sounds—the grunting of the mother owl, the shrill whistles of the lemmings in the tundra, the fluting calls of the swans on the lake, and the whisper of the wind in the grass. It was also filled with smells—the earthy odor of damp moss, the tangy aroma of the apple, and the essence of Kristi . . . roses and honey and woman.

How he wanted to taste her.

Instead, he bit into the apple, chewing it slowly, trying to occupy his hands and mouth as innocently as possible. It was the hardest thing he'd ever made himself do. Every bone and sinew in his body ached to make love with Kristi, and the thought of never making love with her again left him with a chasm deep inside. A chasm no one else could fill. How could he ever leave his love?

The thought depressed him, making him feel suddenly very discouraged, very tired. Flipping the apple core over his shoulder, he covered his mouth to smother a yawn. His eyes slid longingly to her lap. "Sorry about that. I haven't been sleeping very well these past few nights."

"I know. You haven't been snoring."

"Just think. Soon I'll be gone, and you won't have to lie awake and listen to me snore," he said, giving her a soulful look.

Her stomach clenched at the thought of his leaving, and she took one deep breath then another to ease the pain. But nothing would fill the emptiness, she decided as she shifted over to the edge of the blanket. "Why don't you put your head on my lap and take a nap?"

He grinned, looking as pleased as if she'd offered him a golden egg. Quickly he accepted, moving his head around until he found a comfortable place on her lap, then closed his eyes with a sigh of contentment.

Kristi smiled down at him, not in the least taken in by his shenanigans and not in the least bit upset by them either. She wanted an excuse to hold him.

It made her happy just to look at him. He had so

many laughter lines around his eyes, and the creases in his cheeks made her want to smile every time they flashed. Unable to resist the urge, she touched the groove, then trailed her fingers across his cheekbone and began massaging his temple.

"Hmmm. That's nice."

"You're supposed to be sleeping."

"I'm afraid to, in case I miss anything."

She laughed softly. "I'll wake you if Intrepid decides to fly."

"That wasn't what I was afraid of missing."

The longing in his voice stilled her laughter.

Time was running out, and oh, how she'd miss Dev when he was gone. Never before had her life been so full, had so much meaning. His presence added an extra dimension to everything, and her love for him added an extra awareness. When he went south, he'd take the blue out of the sky and the gold from the sun. And his eyes would tug all the green out of the tundra. It would indeed be a bleak barren land without him.

Gradually Kristi became aware that the owlet was shaking his feathers.

"Dev," she whispered. "He's awake."

Dev pushed himself into a sitting position and stared at the ookpik through half-closed lids. Intrepid was hopping up and down and flapping his wings.

"My gosh, I think he is getting serious about this flying business," Dev said, cocking his head to smile at Kristi.

Wishing that her heart wouldn't do such funny things when he smiled at her, Kristi smiled back. When he patted the blanket next to him, she obediently moved closer, and he snaked his arm around her, cuddling her against his side. He felt warm and wonderful, and she knew there was no place on earth she'd rather be than sitting there next to Dev, watching the drama of nature—of survival—unfold. For flight meant survival.

Flight almost meant fulfillment. Would she ever know what it felt like to fly?

Dev drew in a deep breath, waiting, hoping. He'd never expected to actually see the ookpik fledge and couldn't think of anything else he'd rather witness— except the sight of Kristi leaving her own nest to try out her wings.

Intrepid, however, looked as if he would soon master the mystery of flight. Determination quivered in every feather as he flapped his wings and sprang into the air. Two wobbly wingbeats later he was on the ground again.

Go, Intrepid, go, Dev silently urged the little one, wishing he could also urge Kristi to do the same with him.

Shaking his feathers into place, Intrepid spread his wings and tried again. With a run and a hop, he rose into the air, flapping wildly toward them. This time he managed to stay aloft, barely clearing their heads before landing on the outstretched wing of the carved goose.

Turning in unison, Dev and Kristi followed Intrepid's flight, sighing in relief when he landed safely. The owlet stared down at them, his yellow eyes wide with newfound wisdom. Then, before they could move, he leaned forward into the wind, flapped twice, and winged away.

"He did it," Dev yelled, laughing in delight as he hugged Kristi. "He flew."

"Yes. He flew."

The sadness in her voice stilled his laughter as he remembered what the fledging meant. It was time for him to go, and Kristi hadn't offered to come with him.

Rising to his knees, he pulled her around to kneel between his thighs. His hands framed her face, his thumbs gently stroked her cheeks as he smiled down at her. "I don't want to leave you, Kristi," he whispered softly. "I love you."

Kristi's eyes grew wide with wonder. "You love me!"

"Yes, Kristi, I love you," Dev declared, relieved to finally speak the words he'd been aching to say for the last three days.

"But—but you told me you didn't want to fall in love with me."

He smiled at her confusion and leaned over to drop a light kiss on the tip of her nose. "I know, Kristi, and I fought it every step of the way. But I'm afraid I've fallen in love with you."

Slanting his head, he told her again and again with each kiss just how much he loved her.

Kristi matched him kiss for kiss while the words thrummed through her head and her heart. Dev loved her, she loved him. And she'd think about his leaving when the time came.

He raised his head and gazed at her. "I want to make love with you again, Kristi."

Her blue eyes were bright with love. Now wasn't the time for sadness. It was a time for joy. Joy. Laughter. Love.

She gave him a dazzling smile. "Yes, Dev, let's make love."

"Ah, Kristi. Kristi. I wanted this time to be perfect for you. I wanted to love you in a big, comfortable bed."

"This bed is soft," she said, running her fingers through the thick spongy moss. "And it matches your eyes."

"With silk sheets."

Reaching out, she picked up his bomber jacket. "I'll settle for the lining of your jacket. I've grown quite attached to this old thing," she said as she spread it on the ground beneath her and shifted a lumpy pocket out of the way.

He gave her a crooked smile, wondering if it were possible to love her any more than he already did. "And in a warm room."

She gazed out over the tundra—lying bleak, barren, and beautiful beneath the late-afternoon sun—then turned to bathe him in the warmth of her smile. "I can't think of any place I'd rather make love."

She was right, Dev thought. It seemed fitting that they make love in this primitive setting. Everything was reduced to the basics. Man. Woman. Courtship. Mating. Migrating north in the spring, south in the fall.

But he wouldn't think about that now. Now was the time for mating.

"Yes, it's a perfect place for you, my love," he said, pushing all thoughts but one out of his mind.

"Perfect, because you're here to share my joy," she said, her voice low and sultry.

He began by kissing the pulse point at the base of her jaw. The touch of his lips sent shivers of delight down her spine, and she lifted her chin, inviting him to explore further. He trailed a path of sizzling kisses over her throat to the other pulse point, which throbbed in response. Lowering her chin, she offered him the back of her neck. His breath fanned her hair, cooling her flushed skin—skin immediately rewarmed by the heat of his lips as he pressed kiss after fevered kiss against the nape of her neck.

"Hmmm. You're bringing me joy." Slowly, languorously she tilted her head and looked at him, a smile of pure pleasure curving her mouth. Just as slowly she arched her neck and lay it against his. She felt a hint of his whiskers and the scratchy wool of his sweater, but most of all she felt his strength and his goodness. She drew away, then rolled her head to brush the other side of his neck. Back and forth she moved, brushing one side of his neck and then the other, mimicking the swans.

Dev remained motionless, as his heart began pounding and his throat ached with suppressed emotion. Oh, how he loved this woman. He loved her warmth and her sensitivity and her willingness to give.

Finally she raised her head and looked at him, a tremulous smile on her lips. They both laughed breathlessly.

Lips parted, she waited for his kiss, and when it didn't come, she went searching. He pressed his forehead against hers, holding her aloof, afraid that if he so much as touched her lips, he'd lose what was left of his control.

She continued to seek his lips, but he kept them just out of reach. "Oh, Dev!" she said in frustration.

"Hmmm?"

"Hold still."

"Naw."

Kristi reached up to capture his head, but he caught her hands in his and held them outstretched at shoulder height. Pressed together forehead to forehead, hand to hand, and thigh to thigh they swayed back and forth in a dance of courtship, a dance of love—Kristi seeking, Dev evading.

"Kiss me, Dev," Kristi whispered when she couldn't bear it any longer. "Please, kiss me."

He kissed her then, with a passion that sent the blood soaring through her body. She gripped his hands tightly while the world spun like a crazy top. When he finally lifted his lips, her knees were ready to crumble. With a supreme effort, she held herself erect while all she wanted to do was to stretch out with Dev on top of her, inside her.

Dev stared into her eyes as the blood pounded in his ears. Patience, he warned himself. Patience. But where was he going to get the patience . . . the restraint . . . to give Kristi the pleasure she deserved?

"Let's slow down."

"Let's not." Her hands crept under his sweater to cover his chest. She found his flat nipples, flirting with one and then the other until they were hard and erect.

He squeezed her hands through the sweater. "So you wanna play, do you?"

She shook her head, slipping her hands free to push the sweater up his body. "Nope. I want to see you."

With a wide smile, he lifted his arms, allowing her to pull the sweater over his head. Still smiling, he protected his chest with his bent arms as he began unbuttoning her shirt. She waited impatiently until he had removed it, then slipped into his arms, flattening herself against him. Slowly, sensuously, she rubbed her breasts through the thick matt of hair that covered his chest. The hair tickled her skin, stimulating her, arousing her, making her totally aware of their differences and that he was all man.

Dev felt her nipples grow hard against his chest, and with a moan, he wrapped his arms around her. They swayed together, skin to skin, while the sun kissed their shoulders and warmed their bare backs.

She could go on holding him for the rest of the day, Kristi realized, and if she weren't careful, the sun would set before she had a chance to explore him.

"Dev, I want to *see* you," she whispered, as she urged him down onto the blanket. He went willingly, stretching out on his back with her on top.

She lay against him for a moment, then pushed herself to her knees and looked down at him. She'd seen him naked to the waist before but only in the twilight, and both times she'd been too upset to enjoy the experience. Now her gaze roved leisurely over his tanned muscles and trim abdomen. Finally she reached out and threaded her fingers through the springy hair covering his chest, then traced the narrow shaft which harpooned to his waist. It wasn't enough to touch him, and she lowered her head and flicked the tip of her tongue against his nipple.

He drew in a breath, scarcely breathing as her lips found him, then her teeth. After a few moments of sweet torture, she moved to his other nipple, tasting, kissing, nibbling—each movement sending a jolt of pleasure clear through to his manhood.

Slowly she stitched a seam of kisses down the center of his body, tasting the salt, feeling the coolness of his skin, smelling his musky male scent. Reaching his navel, she paused to poke her tongue inside, then pressed her lips in the hollow just above his belt.

His hands caught her head, raising it. "Kristi, sweetheart. You're not playing fair."

"I haven't even begun to play," she warned huskily.

"Well, take it easy or the game will be over."

She eased out of his grasp and found herself staring down at tight jeans stretched even tighter. She looked up at him, a smug feminine smile curving her lips. "What a shame he has to be so uncomfortable. Let me see if I can make him feel better."

Belt buckle loosened, she carefully eased the zipper over his swollen manhood, then slipped her hands inside. He leaned back on his elbows, raising his hips so she could slide the jeans down his legs. His moccasins and socks came, too, leaving him dressed in blue briefs—bulging blue briefs.

She stared at him for long moments. "Have you ever considered modeling briefs?" she asked, thinking back to the day they'd met.

"What!" He shot her a pleased little grin. "Lady, you malign me."

"I think not," she said, as she slowly pulled the briefs in question down his hips. He sprang forth, gorgeously erect. "Oh, Dev, you're magnificent."

And he was. More magnificent than she'd ever imagined. She touched him once—on the tip of his hard shaft—but resisted the urge to touch him again. Already she was damp for him, hot for him. And if she really touched him, she'd deny herself the long awaited pleasure of exploring his body.

Dev lay perfectly still, wishing she would continue to touch him, to caress him. But she was in charge, and he didn't want to spoil her joy. He could only hope she didn't play too long.

Inch by torturous inch she trailed his briefs down, measuring off each inch with a kiss on the insides of both thighs. He murmured in protest and clenched them together, praying for control. His legs received the same attention, as did his ankles, leaving him wishing he was twelve inches shorter one moment and twelve inches longer the next.

When Kristi kissed the arch of his foot, he jerked. She kissed him again. He jerked again, and his legs began trembling. Her eyes danced with mischief: Dev had sensitive feet. Holding his ankle with one hand, she ran her nails along the length of his instep. He made a token attempt to pull away, then waited for her next move. She traced an ever-widening circle on the bottom of his left foot.

"You're playing with fire," he growled in warning.

Looking down his long legs, she realized just how sensitive his feet were. He was straining erect.

"I want to play some more," she said, reveling in the power she had to make him tremble.

Lifting both feet, she pressed them against her breasts, aware of the immediate hardening of her nipples as they thrust against his tender arches. Carefully avoiding his bandaged wound, she began brushing her breasts back and forth against his soles.

Her knees began to shake, although not as bad as his. She laughed huskily, watching shudder after shudder ripple down Dev's legs and through his pelvis. And a throbbing began deep within her.

Dev had never felt such an overwhelming need to be joined with a woman. But not just any woman; he wanted Kristi. Suddenly reaching the end of his tether, he lifted open arms to her. Kristi came willingly, her breasts brushing the hair-roughened insides of his legs as she slid down between them to spread her body flush against his. She lay there, feeling the warmth of his chest against her breasts, wanting very much to feel the warmth of his skin against the rest of her body.

"My turn," Dev said, abruptly rolling her onto his bomber jacket.

Releasing the button of her jeans, he pulled down the zipper. Unable to resist the urge, he slipped his fingers beneath her panties, then dipped them lower to touch her intimately.

She moaned, then sighed, then waited impatiently as he left her to skim her panties and jeans down her legs.

He didn't move, just stared at the golden curls which cloaked her femininity, thinking that she was absolutely exquisite. He swallowed hard.

"A man could spend the rest of his life just looking at you. But I want to do more than look."

She closed her eyes, waiting for him to come to her, the memory of their loving making her warm.

He touched her, not with his hand but with something that whispered across her breast. Now it was there, now it wasn't, each stroke exciting tiny nerve endings she never knew existed. She attempted to raise her head, but he gently pushed her down and trailed the instrument of sweet torture over her other breast.

"Dev," she gasped. "What are you doing to me?"

"Playing."

This time when she lifted her head, she saw the large white plume. "A feather!"

"It came floating down from the heavens so I just had to use it." He laughed softly. "What could be more suitable for my bird lady?"

The feather danced from one nipple to the other, brushing them until they were straining erect and she was writhing.

"But . . . what . . . oh Dev . . . that tickles. Stop. No . . . don't stop."

The feather whispered across her tummy, bringing with it a shower of moonbeams which danced through her to gather in the center of her universe. The intensity of the sensations grew and grew as the feather dipped and swirled and taunted and teased, dropping lower and lower. When it brushed her inner lips she exploded, gasping in wonder as wave after wave of pleasure pulsed through her body.

"Oh Dev . . . Dev . . . Dev."

He leaned over her, watching her, enjoying her passionate reaction to his loving. And when her eyes finally lost their dazed expression, he kissed her.

"So responsive," he breathed against her lips. "So sexy." Another kiss. "So wanton." Raising his head, he gazed down at her. "And I want you now."

"Oh, yes. Please, Dev." Willingly she opened her legs to him.

As he came to her she realized what had been missing moments before. It wasn't enough to experience pleasure alone. She wanted to fly with Dev. To share with him the exaltation of winging high above the land, free of earthly bonds. Of swooping and gliding and rising with the wind. But she needed him before she could fly. Just as he needed her.

Oh, how he needed Kristi, Dev thought, as he buried himself deep inside her warm, welcoming sheath. He needed her inspiration, her strength, her love to make him feel like a King. With Kristi at his side he could go anywhere he wanted to go, do anything he wanted to do, be anything he wanted to be. And all he wanted was to love her, to be hers, to go with her to the ends of the earth and beyond.

Dev came to Kristi again and again, each thrust lifting her higher and higher while she spurred him on to new heights.

She was a bird. He was the wind. Together they soared on wings of love.

Twelve

Dev collapsed into her waiting arms. She held him with tender love as they spiraled slowly to earth.

"Oh, Dev," she whispered. "We flew."

"Yes, Kristi, we flew."

"I never thought I could fly so high or so far, but I did because you were there to inspire me."

He pressed a kiss into the hollow of her throat. "You're so loving, so responsive, Kristi, I couldn't help but be inspired."

Easing over onto his back, he rolled Kristi on top, and with his free hand snagged the blanket up to cover her. It had never happened to him before, this feeling of total commitment to a woman. He had given her every ounce of love he possessed, and he would continue to give it to her for the rest of his life.

They were like the swans, he thought, listening to them calling back and forth to each other on the lake. He was the cob; Kristi the pen. But did she want to be his lifelong mate?

Kristi snuggled against Dev's chest, listening in contentment to his heart beating beneath her ear. It sounded like a grouse drumming its wings, and she thought idly of the other familiar sights and sounds that would remind her of Dev. The snowy owl, the courting swans, the hauntingly sad cry of the loon would all make her think of her dear tenderfoot. Oh, how she'd miss him when he was gone.

With a deep sigh he nuzzled her neck. "It's time to go, Kristi," he said, wishing with all his heart that Kristi would tell him that she loved him.

"Do we have to?" Kristi asked, wanting to keep Dev here with her for the rest of her life.

"I'm afraid so, sweetheart." He sat up, bringing her with him.

His soulful eyes stopped Kristi's heart, and she reached out and gave him a quick hug. He started to say something, thought better of it, and leaned over to pick up their clothes, giving her a weak smile as he faced her again. The smile was a sad replica of the wide one he normally wore, and it made Kristi feel like crying as they dressed in silence, then stood hand in hand on the hilltop.

"I guess they've gone," he said slowly, searching the tundra for the owls.

She shook her head slightly. "They'll continue to use the grave as a home base, but there's no reason why you can't put the marker up now."

"Would you help me move it?" he asked, knowing there was no one else on earth he'd rather share this moment with than Kristi.

"Oh, yes, Dev," she whispered, offering up a prayer of thanks that she was there with Dev, at this time, in this place, standing beside him while he completed his quest.

Helping Dev move the marker was one of the most touching things Kristi had ever done, made more so by Dev's insistence that the Canada goose face south.

"That's the way the King was headed when he crashed, you know. Home to his loved ones."

Where Dev would soon be going, she thought, reaching out to take his hand as he stood, head bowed, saying his silent farewell to his grandfather.

Tears blurred her vision, and she closed her eyes tightly, forcing them back. She was being much too emotional, she chided herself, however, she couldn't help but react to the reverence of the moment, the beauty of their lovemaking, and the realization that Dev no longer had a reason to stay. Well, at least she'd have one more night with him, and she was going to make the most of it, she decided.

Dev pulled her against his chest and wrapped his arms around her.

"I have the feeling grandfather is here with us . . . and has been since the day I arrived." His body swayed slightly as he bent to kiss one side of her neck. "He'd be happy for us. Especially for me." He nuzzled her ear. "Because his being here has led me to you." He shuddered as the old fear resurfaced. "I don't like the idea of you flying around the North, Kristi. You could crash and die, like grandfather did."

"And you could get killed crossing Pennsylvania Avenue."

Dev barely heard her words as the gut-wrenching vision flashed through his mind—of Kristi lying in an unmarked grave somewhere in this lonely, merciless land. Worse yet, no grave at all.

"Please, Kristi, come work with me," he said, his throat aching with concern. "I can't bear the thought of going south and leaving you here."

She pulled back to look at him, and the longing and love in his eyes took her breath away, leaving her almost speechless.

"But, Dev . . . you said that you wouldn't want me to work for you if we made love."

"I know I did, but I'll give up chairing the commission if it means that you'll be safe. I love you, Kristi. I know it's too soon for you to have fallen in love with me, but if we could be together, maybe you—"

Reaching up, she placed her fingers against his lips. "Shhh, Dev. I love you."

He caught her hand and clasped it against his heart. "You love me?" he whispered in disbelief, then whispered it again, louder this time with growing hope. "You love me?"

"Yes, Dev, I love you," she said, her voice ringing with sincerity. "I knew for certain that I loved you when you were flapping your arms, trying to help the little ookpik fly."

He stared down at her a moment longer, then with a sigh of relief, wrapped his arms around her and hugged her close. "Kristi, Kristi," he murmured over and over again into her hair, and when it was no longer enough to just hold her, he released her slightly and kissed her.

Finally, with sighs and tiny kisses, he reluctantly ended the kiss and raised his head to search Kristi's eyes. They were shining with love, the kind of love that melted his insides, that made him dare hope that things would work out all right. "If I could, my darling, I'd give up everything and come work with you," he said.

"Dev, you'd do that for me?" she asked, wondering, for a brief instant, if her dream would come true—the dream of marrying a man who shared her love of wildfowl, who would work beside her in the field, who would help her protect her birds.

"In a minute, Kristi, if it were only me who would be affected by my decision," Dev said, his eyes reflecting the anguish that tore at his soul. "But the Senator and his people are counting on me to take his place. They've worked so hard, and there's so much at stake. I just can't walk away from the responsibility. I can't let them down."

With a sigh, Kristi layed her head against Dev's chest. "I know you can't walk away from your responsibilities, Dev. That it would go against your very nature to let anyone down. It's one of the things I love about you. And it's also the reason I can't stand beside you. You expect too much of people, Dev. Of yourself, of Brenda, of your father, and now me. And I don't want to disappoint you or lose your respect."

Slowly he placed his hand against the side of her neck, then bent his head to rest his forehead against hers. She was so vulnerable, and he was afraid he would shatter the fragile bond they had begun to build between them again.

"Maybe I do expect too much of people, Kristi, but the only reason I'd be disappointed in you is if you chose to stay in your comfortable nest."

"What do you mean?"

"All your life you've been hiding beneath your father's shadow." He took a deep breath, then raised his head again and gazed tenderly into her eyes. "Please don't be angry with me for saying this, Kristi, but isn't it time you went out on your own?"

Kristi stared at Dev, feeling just a little angry despite the hesitancy in his voice. But he *was right*— even her father had said the same thing this spring. However, just because Dev was right didn't mean she was willing to exchange one dependence for another.

"Come work for you and stand in *your* shadow, you mean?"

"I'm not the sun," he said, dropping his hand away. "I am the wind."

He is the wind, she thought, her last shred of anger vanishing. She had flown with Dev in love, perhaps she could also fly with him in life.

Sighing softly, she reached up to slip her hands behind his head. "Oh, Dev, how can I be angry with you when you know my very soul?"

"I know your soul, Kristi, because it is the other half of mine."

She smiled at him in bemusement. "The other half of yours?"

He smiled back, his eyes glowing with conviction. "I believe that every person has a soul mate, Kristi—

like the undefinable bond that keeps the swans together—and my soul belongs to yours."

"And mine to yours," Kristi whispered as she drew his head down and kissed him.

The kiss was an affirmation of their love, and when he finally raised his head, they were both trembling. "You're like the little ookpik—afraid you might fall, but wanting to fly all the same." He kissed her again. "But I know you can, Kristi. I believe in you."

Releasing her, he unzipped his bomber jacket and pulled a jewelry box out of the inside pocket. "I bought this in Fairbanks. It seemed to call out to me, and I now know the reason why," he said, thumbing open the lid. "It symbolizes my love for you."

Kristi took the box in both hands. Inside, on a bed of blue velvet, lay a carved ivory pendant of two swans, one hovering overhead attached by the wingtip to the other, which was sitting on the ground. She stared at it for long moments. Slowly she raised her eyes to Dev's. His green eyes were glowing with love—steadfast, undying love. The kind of love she'd always dreamed of sharing with her mate.

With a smile, he lifted the pendant out of the box and fastened the golden chain around her neck. "I'm waiting for you to fly, my love," he said, his gaze lingering on the swans where they lay nestled in the hollow at the base of her throat.

"Oh, Dev. I don't know what to say."

"Say you'll come south."

She was torn between her love for him and her fear of failure—of failing Dev. "I . . . maybe I will come." Her voice was uncertain, but husky with longing. "I . . . have to think about it some more. There are so many things to sort out. And I still have this project to complete."

"I'm a patient man, Kristi. I'll wait." Lowering his head, he covered the swans briefly with his lips. "But

I can't wait to make love with you again. Let's go home."

Later, as Kristi lay in Dev's bed, snuggled against his warm body, she realized she had been wrong earlier. It wasn't enough to fly with Dev in life. She had to fly alone first. And she would.

Kristi's confidence lasted until the next morning, when the intrusion of a floatplane shattered their arctic paradise.

They were still in bed when it buzzed the camp, still satiated from another session of loving, still so full of each other that they had hardly said a word, except the three most important ones.

With a startled oath, Dev began throwing on his clothes, and Kristi followed suit, knowing in her heart that this could be the beginning of the end. By the time the plane taxied to shore, she had the coffee boiling, and Dev and Rex were down at the beach.

Kristi watched in dismay as Dev led three men toward the camp kitchen. She'd met the pilot before, but the other two—one walking beside Dev carrying an open mike, the other backing ahead of them carrying a rolling camera—made her want to turn tail and run.

"We learned in Fairbanks that Congressman Devlin King from Texas had disappeared into the barren wasteland of northern Alaska, and we decided to come out and see if he was looking for oil or gold," the portly interviewer was saying, obviously in love with the sound of his own voice.

Dev remained silent, feeling as though he were caught between a rock and a hard place. He really didn't want the media to learn why he'd come to Alaska; they'd have a sentimental field day. Nor did he want them to guess why he'd stayed.

"Or are you looking for love?" the interviewer continued as the camera panned to Kristi, who was passing a cup of coffee to the weathered bush pilot. "Do I smell romance in the air?"

Dev felt an overwhelming urge to fix his nose so he'd never smell again.

"Well, Brewer, I didn't come looking for gold or oil," he said easily. "But I have been trying to convince Miss Bjornson to head the Wildfowl Task Force for the commission I'm chairing."

Brewer nodded wisely. "For our viewers' information, that's the commission which is studying the pros and cons of draining the wetlands along the Gulf Coast." He smiled, looking pleased with himself. "The Gulf Coast is a long way from here, Congressman. What made you choose Miss Bjornson for the job? Outside of the fact that she's a beautiful young woman."

Kristi glared at Dev, feeling totally betrayed and about as beautiful as a plucked chicken. He knew how vulnerable she felt about speaking in front of an audience, yet he was forcing her into the limelight. A wave of panic swept through her, leaving her legs trembling. She wanted to run but was afraid to move in case she fell. Instead she leaned against the table, folded her arms across her chest, and listened to the charming congressman with the silver tongue.

"Miss Bjornson may be young and beautiful, but she's also eminently qualified in her field," Dev said easily, his smile hiding his growing unease. "She's done major research projects on wildfowl all over the North, has publishing credits longer than your arm, and knows her subject inside out. I'm satisfied that I couldn't find anyone better for the job."

"And what have you to say about this, Kristi? May I call you Kristi?" The silky smile Brewer gave her made her toes curl.

Kristi stared at the microphone Brewer waved under her nose, unable to think of one single, solitary thing to say. She touched the pendant nervously, then hastily dropped her hand away. Would they realize the significance of the swans? Worse yet, would they know she and Dev had been making love all night? *They had to know*. And they *had* to be thinking that Dev was offering her the job because she was his lover.

"I haven't d-decided to t-take the job yet," she stammered.

"And I've decided that I don't want Kristi for the task force," Dev said softly, his voice full of love. "I want her for my wife."

Kristi gazed at Dev in horror, wanting to dig a hole in the permafrost and bury herself. How could he stand there and calmly announce to this obnoxious man that he wanted to marry her.

"My, my, I was right. I did smell romance. My congratulations, Kristi. I'm sure you'll be much happier being a congressman's wife than studying a bunch of dumb birds. They're only good for one thing." Brewer patted his stomach, his expression making it very clear what he thought should be done with the birds. "The farmers need the land. People have to be fed."

Suddenly Kristi's dumb horror turned into burning rage, and she let Brewer have it with both barrels. Her first volley of words scattered like buckshot, and she bit her lips frustrated at her failure to make herself clear. Taking a deep breath, she regrouped and fired again.

"Because you like to eat, they've created a selenium disaster in the San Joaquin Valley and contaminated millions of acres of wetland habitat." Hands on hips she glared at him. "Because you like to eat, they're plowing up nesting grounds so they can plant a few more acres of grain." With chin out and eyes blazing, she advanced on Brewer, stabbing home her points with her words as well as with her forefinger at his paunch. "Because you like to eat, they drain reservoirs to irrigate Idaho potato fields and strand loon chicks before they can fly." She stabbed again. "What's going to happen when the well-fed people can't hear the geese on the wing or the cry of the loon?"

Dev stood aside, glowing with pride. Warmed up to her subject and in full battle, Kristi was a sight to behold. Brewer retreated, and she kept advancing, firing fact after fact as she backed him up against her tent. A pair of jeans flapped around Brewer's head, and Dev was pleased when the camera captured that image for posterity.

Kristi's voice softened as she talked about the importance of preserving the land, keeping it safe for all of God's creatures. While she talked, she surveyed her domain, her face glowing with a mixture of love and fierce determination to protect it. When she'd finished stating her case, she turned without apology and stomped back to the camp kitchen.

Watching her, Dev wanted to jump up and down and cheer. Instead he nonchalantly rocked back on his heels, a hand covering his mouth. It wouldn't do to look too impressed.

The grinning pilot drained his coffee, set it on the table, and applauded, while Rex threw in a couple barks of approval.

"Well, I guess you told me," the interviewer said, trying to recover his aplomb. "But I'm afraid it's not what we were after."

"Oh, yes we were," the cameraman said, lowering his camera as he approached Kristi. "An interview right from the heart." He shook hands with Kristi, who stared at him with a dazed expression on her face. "This happens to be my production, Miss Bjornson, and I'll see that we do right by you." Turning, he extended his hand to Dev. "Congressman. A pleasure to meet you again, sir." He looked regretfully at the coffeepot. "Sorry we can't stay for coffee, but we're on a tight schedule."

As Kristi watched them climb into the plane, the

adrenaline that had kept her going through the interview suddenly fled, leaving her trembling with despair.

Forcing back the tears that stung her eyes, she swung on Dev. "And you might as well go too."

Thirteen

Dev stared at Kristi in surprise. Then surprise turned to concern as he recognized the pigeon-staring-at-a-hawk expression on her face. "What's the matter, Kristi?" he asked quietly.

"Why did you tell that man you wanted to marry me?" she cried out as the feelings of disbelief, disappointment, and dismay threatened to overwhelm her again. What should have been the happiest moment in her life had turned into a nightmare.

Dev smiled at her. "Because it's the truth, and I don't care if the whole world knows it."

"Well, thousands of people will see it on TV and wonder why you'd want to marry a woman who made a blathering fool of herself."

"Kristi, you didn't. You were terrific."

He reached out to touch her, but Kristi brushed his hand away, along with his praise. She knew better. She's been the panic-stricken speaker, searching frantically for words. Like Intrepid, she'd flapped her wings and had fallen flat on her face.

"I stuttered and repeated myself. I sounded like an empty-headed birdbrain."

She started to turn away but Dev gripped her shoulders, refusing to let her go. "You impressed a hard-hearted cameraman, and I was so proud of you, I wanted to cheer."

"You're prejudiced. Besides, it's all your fault this happened. You knew how much I hate being in the spotlight, yet you deliberately pushed me front and center, then made a statement that blew me out of the water."

"I'm sorry I blurted out the proposal like that, Kristi," he said, his eyes begging for understanding. "But it was the only way I could think of to protect you."

"Protect me! From what?"

"Brewer was looking for a hot gossip item, and I wasn't about to provide him with one, especially when it involved the woman I want beside me for the rest of my life."

The thought that he might not have Kristi beside him for the rest of his days returned suddenly, threatening to tear him apart. He had survived Brenda's departure, but life without Kristi would be a wasteland.

Slowly he released her shoulders and stepped back, staring blindly at his hands, which were as empty as his heart. "I thought you loved me, too, but maybe I was wrong. Maybe you don't love me enough to spend a lifetime with me."

The anguish in his voice chased away all her thoughts but one. "Oh, Dev, I do love you. I do want to spend a lifetime with you," she said, moving forward to throw her arms around him and pull him close.

With a sigh of relief, Dev bent his head to nestle his neck against hers. "Thank God," he whispered into her hair as the sense of impending doom retreated once more. He kissed her then, a soul-deep kiss, a kiss which spoke the vows straight from his heart. He'd take care of Kristi, keep her safe for the rest of her life.

Kristi heard the vows as clearly as if he'd spoken

them aloud. Heard them and allowed herself to hope . . . for a few wistful moments while she returned his kisses. She loved Dev and wanted to be his wife more than anything in the world but . . .

Finally, reluctantly, Dev raised his head and gazed down at her, his eyes brimming with love. "I realize it won't be easy for you to live in Washington, to be the wife of a congressman, but I know you can do it."

Kristi gazed back, smiling bravely as she clung to her hope. "After following Dad around the lecture circuit for years, I guess I can hold my own in the cocktail crowd."

"I have no doubts that you could hold your own with anyone, sweetheart, even the President. And you're so beautiful, you'd outshine every woman in sight. I'd be so proud to have you on my arm."

She drew in a deep sigh of happiness, feeling so loved, so cherished, and for a few more heartbeats she just stood there and smiled at Dev. Then she sighed again. "But I won't be completely happy unless I'm working with my birds, studying them, protecting them. And if I did marry you, I couldn't work for the commission. I know you said you'd give up being the chairman, but I couldn't let you. It means too much to your political future."

"Oh, Kristi, sweetheart, just when I think I've reached the limits of my love for you, you say something to make me love you more." He trailed his fingers along her cheek, then curled them beneath her jaw. "You could go down to the Chesapeake. There's enough work there to keep you busy for a lifetime."

"A hundred lifetimes," Kristi said, turning her head slightly to kiss his knuckles. Oh, how she loved this man, this dear, dear tenderfoot.

He brushed his thumb across her lips and continued to smile at her, feeling as though a great weight had been lifted from his shoulders. "And to tell you the truth, I'd be much happier if you were close by.

I'd worry about you if you were down on the Gulf Coast. This way I can keep an eye on you."

Kristi heard his words, heard the love and concern in his voice—and also heard the death knell of her hope. She closed her eyes tightly, trying unsuccessfully to hold back the tears, and when she opened her lids again, they shimmered in her eyes.

"What's the matter, Kristi?" he asked huskily, catching one tear on the tip of his finger even as another escaped and rolled down her cheek.

"I'll live with you in Washington, Dev, but I also have to come north for a few months every year. I love Alaska; it's in my blood," she said, the muscles of her throat so tight with pain, she could barely speak. "I . . . I don't want to make the same mistake my mother made and marry the man I love, only to have to leave him because I couldn't live with him." She swallowed hard and looked up at him. "Because I would eventually have to leave you, Dev, or I'd wither and die."

He stared down at her in dismay as he felt the tenuous bond which held them together begin to give. "Wither and die! Kristi, I've just spent the last five days and nights encouraging you to stretch and grow . . . to rise to new challenges—"

"And you've been worrying about me since the moment we met. What if I'd crashed? What if I'd cut my foot? What if the wolverine had attacked me?"

"Dammit, Kristi, I have good reason to worry about you. Any one of those things could have happened to you." With a groan, he clutched her to his chest.

She pushed against him, and after a moment he reluctantly loosened his hold but still wouldn't let her go.

"I've worked in the North for years, Dev, and nothing has happened to me. Nor is anything likely to happen if I worked in the Chesapeake or on the Gulf Coast, but you'd worry just the same." From somewhere deep inside she dredged up enough strength to move out of his embrace. "You've been trying to protect me from the moment you arrived and you'll probably still be trying to protect me when I'm in my rocker. But I don't need your protection, Dev, and I'm afraid you'll surround me in so many layers of feathers that you'll smother me."

"Kristi, I . . . I—" He reached out to her, but she stepped back.

"I love you, Dev, and if we were married, I'd stand by you whenever you needed me." She brushed away her tears. "But what would happen next spring if I wanted to fly north with the swans? Who do you take after, Dev, your grandmother or your father? Would you let me go freely or would you resent it every time I left?"

"I don't know," he whispered honestly, as her questions hit home. For the first day he'd known how much she loved the North, and from the first day he'd also known how much he hated the thought of her flying around there all by herself. "I just want to keep you safe."

She stared through his unguarded eyes, directly into his soul. The longing she saw there frightened her, shaking her to the core but also firming her resolve. If she did give in to his plea, she would destroy herself and, worse yet, eventually destroy Dev.

Kristi closed her eyes, wishing the world would come to an end, right there and then, so she'd always be with Dev. But it wouldn't, she knew, and she'd go on living. "Just leave, Dev. Please, just go home where you belong," she whispered.

He stared at her for a long, heartrending moment. "I'll leave, if that's what you want, but if you don't come south with the swans, I'll be back," he said, his voice husky with unshed tears. "Because my soul belongs to yours, Kristi." Slowly he raised his hand and touched the pendant he'd placed around her neck. "And I'm waiting for you to fly."

Turning, he crossed the sand toward his tent, head down, shoulders slumped. Through a veil of tears, she watched him go, then climbed into her plane and fired up the engine.

There was no way she could watch Devlin King fly out of her life.

Dev heard the roar of the engine and crammed his shirt into his duffel bag, then stuffed his jeans on top, not allowing himself to think. Because if he began thinking, he'd never make himself leave. And leave he must. For Kristi's sake.

Not thinking lasted until he began rolling up his sleeping bag. The scent of roses brought him to his knees as memories washed over him. Memories of Kristi glowing in the lamplight, moving above him in time to their music, flying with him to the heavens where they had been one—not only in body but in heart and mind and soul.

And memories of how he felt afterward when he'd held her in his arms. So strong, so protective—as if he could take on the world. But only if Kristi were at his side.

Dev stirred only when Rex crawled into the tent and poked his head under his arm. Absently Dev patted the dog, then resumed packing. Rex remained beside Dev while he emptied and collapsed the tent, then followed him back and forth as he hauled his things down to the plane. As Dev loaded his gear, Rex lay with his chin on his outstretched paws, his tail curled over his back, watching with sad brown eyes.

Just before he shoved the plane off the beach, Dev dropped to his knees beside the husky. "Take care of your mistress, Rex," he said, scratching the dog's ear.

Rex whined, and Dev gathered the husky into his arms and held him close, wishing the dog were

Kristi. Rex's tongue flicked out to lick his face. With a soft laugh Dev drew back and patted Rex again, before reaching into his jacket pocket for a tissue.

As he pulled it out, a long white feather floated gently to the ground. Picking it up, Dev held it in the palm of his hand and stared at it while the wind whispered a message in his ears.

Love should lie lightly like a feather.

That was where he'd made his mistake, Dev realized. He was so afraid that something would happen to Kristi that he had tried to tie her to him with bonds of love. Invisible bonds, unexplainable bonds, but bonds just the same. Not like the bonds of nature that made a pen and cob mate for life.

But he could never tie Kristi to him. His love must lie lightly like a feather, allowing her to be free.

And when she finally fledged, he could only hope she would fly south to him.

Somewhere between no-man's-land and the end of the world Kristi calmed down enough to realize just what she'd done.

She had let her one chance at happiness slip out of her life without a fight. She'd fight tooth and nail for her birds, if they were threatened. Why hadn't she fought harder for her love?

Tears still blurred her vision, and when she turned her head to wipe her eyes on her sleeve, she caught sight of Dev's cameras in the rear seat of the plane. In her rush to escape she'd flown off before he'd had a chance to retrieve them.

Maybe she could contact him, she thought, switching on her radio. When he didn't respond to her calls, she turned the plane toward King's Lake, hoping he'd stopped there before heading for Fairbanks. There was no way she could catch his faster plane with hers.

The empty lake dashed her hopes and made her heart ache.

Dev had left without the pictures of the grave marker for his grandmother. He loved the Duchess dearly and was going to be extremely disappointed to arrive home empty-handed. Well, that was one thing she could do for him, Kristi decided, bringing the plane around for a landing.

At the gravesite, Kristi didn't allow herself to think as she adjusted the settings on the cameras. She needed all her concentration not to ruin the pictures.

After shooting all the unexposed film, she sank down beside the wooden Canada goose, finally giving in to her sorrow and regret. Wrapping her arms around her knees, she bowed her head and rocked back and forth.

Dev should be the one taking the pictures. This quest had meant so much to him—and she had ruined it. He had been so kind, so considerate, so loving, and she'd thrown his love back in his face.

He was a keeper. And she had thrown him away.

A high plaintive sound split the silence, like the song a swan sings before it dies. But a swan wasn't singing its death song, Kristi knew. The sound had come from deep inside her soul. Her chest grew tight, her throat began to hurt, and still she sang her anguish.

She had found her mate. How was she ever going to survive without Dev?

It was a long time before Kristi roused herself and flew back to camp. The empty spot where Dev's tent had sat and Rex's sad eyes only intensified her feeling of loneliness, and sometime during the endless night that followed, she decided to fly out to Fairbanks on the off chance Dev would still be there. The least she could do was tell him how much she loved him. And if he'd already left, she'd send him the film and cameras Air Express. Decision made, she finally dozed.

• • •

She woke to fog. Thick fog that trapped her tiny world and made her want to scream in frustration. Silent fog that made her achingly aware of the loneliness of the North.

During the fog-filled week that followed, Kristi paced the beach, listening to the lonesome loons while she searched her soul. Her only comfort was the attentive dog, the ivory pendant, and the tiny white-gold flower she'd found in her tally book. By the time the fog lifted, she had come to terms with herself and what she wanted—no, needed—to do.

She'd go south to see Dev and give their love another chance. And if Dev still wanted her to marry him, she'd accept with the knowledge that they could face their problems and work them out. After all, weren't they both crusaders? Together, they could conquer anything.

But first she had to finish the final count before the swans also flew south. If the research project wasn't completed, they wouldn't be paid, and she couldn't let her father down no matter how desperately she wanted to rush to Dev.

Three weeks later, Kristi flew home to Cordova, happy to leave the silent North. Even the Lady on the Mountain had donned a fresh coat of snow to welcome her, Kristi noted as she pointed the nose of her floatplane at the snowfield on Mount Eccles. She smiled for the first time in weeks.

"We're home, Rex," she told her companion, who was occupying the front seat of the loaded plane. Hearing his name, Rex sat up and looked out the side window.

Landing the plane on Eyak Lake, she taxied in behind the spit and cut the engine. As she stepped ashore she was enveloped in her father's one-arm bear hug. The tall blond-haired man still exuded strength even as he braced himself with one crutch.

"It's great to see you, Kris," Ken Bjornson said, releasing Kristi to give the tail-wagging Rex a quick pat on the head.

Kristi stood back to look at him. " And you, too, Dad. How are you?"

"Fine, fine." Arm in arm they shuffled out of the way of a grizzled old-timer who drove up in his truck to refuel Kristi's plane. "As you can see, they've still got me hog-tied to this cast. It's coming off next week, but I'm getting hog-tied again right away. Mary has agreed to put up with me in my old age."

Kristi gave him another hug. "Oh, Dad. I'm so pleased for you. It's about time you saw the light and asked her to marry you." She released him and smiled up at him again. "But what are you doing here? I thought you'd still be up at the lodge."

"Couldn't stay long. Confounded doctor wanted me back for a checkup, and Mary made me toe the line. Good thing I came home, though. Otherwise I'd have missed all the excitement." He gave Kristi a speculative look. "I hear King needs you."

"Who? Duke?" Duke was the only King her father had met. What would he need her for?

"No. His brother. That congressman."

"How do you know about Dev?" Kristi asked in surprise, trying not to look guilty.

"Saw you both on the TV special. Are you going to marry him?"

She sucked in a ragged breath, trying to loosen the tight vise that gripped her chest. "I don't know, Dad. I hope so, but I just don't know."

He patted her shoulder, started to say something, then patted her shoulder again. "Well, you sure made your old man proud, Kristen." He beamed at her. "I knew you could give a humdinger of a speech if you put your mind to it. You've been getting phone calls from all over—old friends wanting to congratulate you, people offering you jobs, but I didn't know if you'd be available. Were you thinking of working for the congressman, Kris?"

"I told Dev no, but . . ."

"Probably just as well you didn't accept the offer." Ken's blue eyes looked as innocent as a newborn babe's. "At the rate things are going, there might not be a job."

"What do you mean?" Kristi asked in concern.

"They said on the tube that they might cancel the funding for the commission. They've been having hearings all week. Tomorrow's the last day. But they've already heard from a lot of powerful lobbyists—hey, where are you going?" Kristi had broken out of his arms and was trotting toward her plane.

"To Anchorage. To catch the evening flight. Phone and ask them to hold the jet," she called to her father, as she climbed into the Cessna. "I have to be in Washington tomorrow." She didn't know if she could help Dev, but she had to try. Her place was by his side.

"I'll phone Frank and tell the old reprobate you're coming. The least he can do is look after one of his constituents when she comes to the capitol." The last was lost in the whirr of the starter.

Dev glanced from the speaker who sat at a small table before him, both ways down the conference table, trying to determine how the man's words were affecting his four colleagues. He felt as though he'd been through the war, and he still wasn't sure if he was winning.

The battle had been bloody, with the lobbyists bringing in their high-powered guns—like the man who was presently speaking into the microphone—but on the whole, he'd been able to parry their shots.

Surprisingly, support had come from a group of

Texas oilmen and businessmen, spearheaded by Duke, with his father giving silent weight by his mere presence.

Dev's gaze swept past the speaker to the crowded room beyond. There they sat—the Duke, the Duchess, and his mother, who was holding her husband's hand. Dare would've been there, too, if he wasn't in Alberta, but he'd sent another one of his presents—a peace pipe.

Dev was thankful he'd made peace with his father as soon as he'd returned from the North. The Baron still held his body ramrod straight, but there was a slackness about his muscles that bespoke of his recent illness. The realization that his father was mortal had given Dev a shock.

But the Duchess was something else, he thought, his eyes shifting to the fine-boned, firm-skinned, still-beautiful woman who sat between his father and Duke. She had insisted on coming to the hearings, and Dev loved her for it.

All his loved ones were there. Except for Kristi. If only she were by his side, his life would be complete.

Damn. If he didn't start paying attention, he'd blow his chances of getting this commission off the ground. Making a determined effort, he concentrated on the speaker while he mentally counted the ayes and nays. They were pretty much even.

He just needed that something extra to push the balance in his favor.

Having answered the final question to everyone's satisfaction, the man replaced the microphone, collected his papers, and moved to his seat at the back of the room. At that moment the door opened and Frank Tooley, the congressman from Alaska, entered. He nodded at Dev.

Calling a five-minute recess, Dev followed Frank out into the corridor. "What's up?" he asked, wondering why his friend and staunch supporter had deserted him this morning.

"You'll see." Opening the door to an adjacent office, Frank pushed Dev inside. "I'll hold the fort," he said, closing the door behind him.

Dev stared at the woman in the middle of the empty room and felt as if the sun had finally begun to shine again. Kristi flew across the floor toward him, and he caught her to him, swinging her off her moccasined feet.

"You came. Oh, Kristi, my love, you came," he cried, his lips covering hers in a grateful kiss.

"I would've come sooner," Kristi said breathlessly when he finally released her lips. "But I just found out yesterday that you needed me."

He rested is head against her temple. "You're here, Kristi, and that's all that really matters."

She gave him a hug, then stepped back to gaze earnestly into his eyes. "I don't know if I can help, Dev, but I'm willing to try."

"You mean you'll speak before the commission." A wide, beautiful smile creased his cheeks, then faded. "The room is crowded with people."

"I know, but I'm here to speak just the same," she said, looking so brave and determined that he felt as if his heart would burst with love for her.

"Kristi, sweetheart. You don't have to prove you love me." He swept her back into his arms for a quick hug, then released her. "You'd make me the happiest man in the world if you'd just marry me. I promise you can go north as often as you want. I'll come with you whenever I can, and we'll take our children up at least—"

She stopped his words with a long sweet kiss. "Oh, Dev, I want to marry you, to have your children, to be by your side when we're old and gray. But . . ."

"But you're afraid I'll try to hold you too close," he finished for her. His voice grew husky as he continued. "And I don't blame you, Kristi, because I *was* trying to bind you to me. I won't do that ever again. You see, I learned something the day you flew out of my life." Removing a long white feather from his jacket pocket, he released it, letting it flutter down to the palm of his other hand. "From now on, my love will lie as lightly as this feather," he whispered.

Kristi glanced from the feather to the man who held it—and believed him. "I'll be proud to marry you, Dev," she said softly. "As soon as we get your commission funded."

He nestled his free hand against her neck. "It would be a great help if you would speak to the commission, Kristi, but you don't have—"

"But I must." She drew away again, clasping his hand to her lips as she whispered, "You were right, too, Dev. I have to stretch my wings and fly. For me."

Dev stared down into her beautiful face, noting with concern the purple shadows under her blue eyes. Then he smiled in relief. Despite her fatigue, Kristi's eyes were shining with a bright light. She was ready to go to battle—for him.

Frank rapped on the door, then opened it. "Time's up, Commissioner. Better wipe that love-struck look off your mug and call the hearing to order. Our little Kristi is going to make them change their minds."

Kristi's mind went blank as Dev and Frank ushered her into the conference room. There were so many people, she thought in mounting panic when Dev left her at the table and walked to his seat.

Kristi sank into the chair Frank held for her and risked a quick glance at the spectators. Suddenly the walls of the room began closing in on her, and her heart started thumping with dread.

"Mr. Chairman, I know it's highly irregular, but I'd like to request permission for one of my constituents to speak," Frank said, his voice booming above the interested stirrings of the audience. "Miss Bjornson has just arrived from Alaska and has some valuable information which she wishes to bring to your attention. I'm sure what she has to say will have a great bearing on your . . ."

Kristi lost track of Frank's words as she concentrated on breathing slowly, deeply, and pushing back the walls.

"Thank you for coming, Miss Bjornson," Dev said, willing her to look at him.

I love you, his heart called out to her.

Almost as if she had heard him, she raised her blue eyes. They were full of terror.

"As many of you know, I've been trying to recruit Miss Bjornson to work for the commission," Dev continued, trying to give Kristi time to compose herself. "But let me assure you that her presence here today is as much of a surprise to me as it is to you." He gave her his best smile. "Whenever you're ready, Kristi."

Kristi continued to stare at Dev, speechless, as the words she'd carefully written and rehearsed on the red-eye flight from Seattle deserted her. She even forgot to look at her notes. All she could think about was that she must not fail Dev.

Dev's smile widened, creasing his cheeks, giving her courage. Then the congressman from Texas did something that made the audience twitter and kept Washington talking for weeks.

He bent his hands to his shoulders and flapped his elbows!

I believe in you, his eyes told her. *You can do it.*

Kristi heard his silent words as clearly as she could see Dev encouraging the little owlet to fly. A smile trembled on her lips . . . while deep inside a wind swept through her, lifting her heart and giving her courage.

I am the wind, Dev had said.

Her smiled broadened as she touched the pendant at the base of her throat. *I love you,* she told him silently.

I love you, Kristi. And I'm waiting for you to fly.

Dev flapped again.

Picking up the microphone, Kristi spread her wings and soared.

THE EDITOR'S CORNER

◆ Late-Breaking News ◆

The Delaney dynasty continues!
THE DELANEY CHRISTMAS CAROL
by Kay Hooper, Iris Johansen, and Fayrene Preston.
Three NEW stories of Delaney Christmases
past, present, and future.

On sale in paperback from Bantam FANFARE
in November.

◆

There's a kind of hero we all love, the kind who usually wears irresistible tight jeans and holds a less-than-glamorous job. The world doesn't always sing his praises, but the world couldn't do without him—and next month LOVESWEPT salutes him with MEN AT WORK. In six fabulous new romances that feature only these men on the covers, you'll meet six heroes who are unique in many ways, yet are all hardworking, hard-driving, and oh, so easy to love!

First, let Billie Green sweep you away to Ireland, where you'll meet a hunk of a sheep farmer, Keith Donegal. He's the **MAN FROM THE MIST**, LOVESWEPT #564, and Jenna Howard wonders if his irresistible heat is just a spell woven by the land of leprechauns. But with dazzling kisses and thrilling caresses, Keith sets out to prove that the fire between them is the real thing. The magic of Billie's writing shines through in this enchanting tale of love and desire.

In **BUILT TO LAST** by Lori Copeland, LOVESWEPT #565, the hero, Bear Malone, is exactly what you would expect from his name—big, eye-catching, completely fascinating, and with a heart to match his size. A carpenter, he renovates houses for poor families, and he admires the feisty beauty Christine Brighton for volunteering for the job. Now, if he can only convince her that they should make a home and a family of their own . . . Lori makes a delightful and sensual adventure out of building a house.

You'll get plenty of **MISCHIEF AND MAGIC** in Patt Bucheister's new LOVESWEPT, #566. Construction worker Phoenix Sierra knows all about mischief from his friends' practical jokes, and when he lands in an emergency room because of one, he finds magic in Deborah Justin. The copper-haired doctor is enticing, but before she will love Phoenix, he must reveal the vulnerable man hiding behind his playboy facade. You'll keep turning the pages as Patt skillfully weaves this tale of humor and passion.

Kimberli Wagner returns to LOVESWEPT with **A COWBOY'S TOUCH,** LOVESWEPT #567, and as before, she is sure to enchant you with her provocative writing and ability to create sizzling tension. In this story, Jackie Stone ends up working as the cook on her ex-husband's ranch because she desperately needs the money. But Gray Burton has learned from his mistakes, and he'll use a cowboy's touch to persuade Jackie to return to his loving arms. Welcome back, Kim!

There can't be a more perfect—or sexy—title for a book in which the hero is an electric lineman than **DANGEROUS IN THE DARK** by Terry Lawrence, LOVESWEPT #568. Zach Young is a lineman for the county, the one to call when the lights go out. When he gets caught in an electric storm, he finds shelter in Candy Wharton's isolated farmhouse. He makes Candy feel safe in the dark; the danger is in allowing him into her heart. All the stirring emotions that you've come to expect from Terry are in this fabulous story.

Olivia Rupprecht gives us a memorable gift of love with **SAINTS AND SINNERS,** LOVESWEPT #569. Matthew

Peters might be a minister, but he's no saint—and he's determined to get to know gorgeous Delilah Sampson, who's just moved in across the street from his Iowa church. He's as mortal as the next man, and he can't ignore a woman who's obviously in trouble . . . or deny himself a taste of fierce passion. Once again, Olivia delivers an enthralling, powerful romance.

On sale this month from FANFARE are four breathtaking novels. **A WHOLE NEW LIGHT** proves why Sandra Brown is a *New York Times* bestselling author. In this story, widow Cyn McCall wants to shake up her humdrum life, but when Worth Lansing asks her to spend a weekend with him in Acapulco, she's more than a little surprised—and tempted. Worth had always been her friend, her late husband's business partner. What will happen when she sees him in a whole new light?

Award-winning author Rosanne Bittner sets **THUNDER ON THE PLAINS** in one of America's greatest eras—the joining of the East and West by the first transcontinental railroad. Sunny Landers is the privileged daughter of a powerful railroad magnate. Colt Travis is the half-Indian scout who opens her eyes to the beauty and danger of the West . . . and opens her heart to love.

INTIMATE STRANGERS is a gripping and romantic time-travel novel by Alexandra Thorne. On vacation in Santa Fe, novelist Jane Howard slips into a flame-colored dress and finds herself transported to 1929, in another woman's life, in her home . . . and with her husband.

Critically acclaimed author Patricia Potter creates a thrilling historical romance with **LIGHTNING**. During the Civil War, nobody was a better blockade runner for the South than Englishman Adrian Cabot, but Lauren Bradly swore to stop him. Together they would be swept into passion's treacherous sea, tasting deeply of ecstasy and the danger of war.

Also on sale this month, in the hardcover edition from Doubleday, is **SINFUL** by Susan Johnson. Sweeping from the majestic manors of England to the forbidden salons of a Tunisian harem, this is a tale of desperate deception and sensual pleasures between a daring woman and a passionate nobleman.

Happy reading!

With best wishes,

Nita Taublib
Associate Publisher
LOVESWEPT and FANFARE

The Delaney Dynasty lives on in

The Delaney Christmas Carol

by Kay Hooper, Iris Johansen, & Fayrene Preston

Three of romantic fiction's best-loved authors present the changing face of Christmas spirit—past, present, and future—as they tell the story of three generations of Delaneys in love.

<u>CHRISTMAS PAST</u> by Iris Johansen

From the moment he first laid eyes on her, Kevin Delaney felt a curious attraction for the ragclad Gypsy beauty rummaging through the attic of his ranch at Killara. He didn't believe for a moment her talk of magic mirrors and second-sight, but something about Zara St. Cloud stirred his blood. Now, as Christmas draws near, a touch leads to a kiss and a gift of burning passion.

<u>CHRISTMAS PRESENT</u> by Fayrene Preston

Bria Delaney had been looking for Christmas ornaments in her mother's attic, when she saw him in the mirror for the first time—a stunningly handsome man with sky-blue eyes and red-gold hair. She had almost convinced herself he was only a dream when Kells Braxton arrived at Killara and led them both to a holiday wonderland of sensuous pleasure.

<u>CHRISTMAS FUTURE</u> by Kay Hooper

As the last of the Delaney men, Brett returned to Killara this Christmastime only to find it in the capable hands of his father's young and beautiful widow. Yet the closer he got to Cassie, the more Brett realized that the embers of their old love still burned and that all it would take was a look, a kiss, a caress, to turn their dormant passion into an inferno.

 The best in Women's Fiction from Bantam FANFARE. On sale in November 1992 AN 428 8/92

FANFARE

On Sale in July

A WHOLE NEW LIGHT

☐ 29783-X $5.99/6.99 in Canada
by Sandra Brown

<u>New York Times</u> bestselling author

Under the romantic skies of Acapulco, Cyn McCall and Worth Lansing succumb to blazing passion in one reckless moment, and must face the fears and doubts that threaten to shatter their new and fragile bond.

THUNDER ON THE PLAINS

☐ 29015-0 $5.99/6.99 in Canada
by Rosanne Bittner

"Emotional intensity and broad strokes of color...a strong historical saga and a powerful romance. Ms. Bittner [is] at the top of her form."
-- <u>Romantic Times</u>

INTIMATE STRANGERS

☐ 29519-5 $4.99/5.99 in Canada
by Alexandra Thorne

"Talented author Alexandra Thorne has written a complex and emotionally intense saga of reincarnation and time travel, where it just might be possible to correct the errors of time." -- <u>Romantic Times</u>

LIGHTNING

☐ 29070-3 $4.99/5.99 in Canada
by Patricia Potter

Their meeting was fated. Lauren Bradley was sent by Washington to sabotage Adrian Cabot's Confederate ship...he was sent by destiny to steal her heart. Together they are swept into passion's treacherous sea.

☐ Please send me the books I have checked above. I am enclosing $ _____ (add $2.50 to cover postage and handling). Send check or money order, no cash or C. O. D.'s please.

Mr./ Ms. _____

Address _____

City/ State/ Zip _____

Send order to: Bantam Books, Dept. FN 59, 2451 S. Wolf Rd., Des Plaines, IL 60018

Allow four to six weeks for delivery.

Prices and availability subject to change without notice.

 THE SYMBOL OF GREAT WOMEN'S FICTION FROM BANTAM

Ask for these books at your local bookstore or use this page to order. FN 59 8/92